AUTHOR OF THE SECRETS OF GABRIEL

ZENTS SOWUNMI

UNEQUALLY

YOKING

A NOVEL

UNEQUALLY

YOKING

BY

ZENTS

SOWUNMI

For additional copies of this or other titles by Zents Sowunmi, write to Korloki Publishers Inc., (a subsidiary of Allzents Groups Inc., Mastic Beach, New York 11951. Please allow 4 to 6 weeks for delivery. For bulk orders contact us via email korlokipublishers@gmail.com

UNEQUALLY YOKING

KORLOKI An imprint of Korloki Publishers Inc. Mastic Beach LI NY 11951 USA

UNEQUALLY YOKING

Cover design: Vick Tracey Private Designer

Interior design: Korloki Publishers Inc.

Photographs: Vick Tracey Private Designer

Summary: Passionately powerful and provocative love and crime scenes within the
                       Church that extended beyond the two continents.

ISBN: 9781936739226

PRINTED IN USA

DEDICATION

My Buddies,

My cherished secrets

Hidden memories,

My first love

ZENTS

SOWUNMI

UNEQUALLY

YOKING

KORLOKI PUBLISHERS INC.

New York. London. Lagos. Shanghai. Toronto

Resounding praises for the Oracle, International

Best Selling Author

ZENTS SOWUNMI

A super story maker and a teller of our time

Dr. Adeyemi, Lagos. Nigeria

Zents ability to bring the story to your doorstep is

exceptionally unique.

Jacky Vasquez, Brooklyn NY

The Oracle Zents is quite a spot to read.

Dauda Shokeye, Bronx NY

Zents, the master at mixing reality of our time with the

fiction of events.

Lanre Tejuosho, Maryland MD

Deeply intriguing

Susan West, Memphis TN

Very daring and Creative

Susan Anderson, Dallas Texas

Do not miss these exciting books from bestselling Author

ZENTS KUNLE SOWUNMI

- ❖ *The Vultures and Vulnerable*
- ❖ *President Obama: Hero or villain of Capitalism?*
- ❖ *Ogun State Policy of Manipulation*
- ❖ *Before the Journey Became Home*
- ❖ *100 ways to Laugh*
- ❖ *Cien Maneras de Reir*
- ❖ *The Gatecrashers*
- ❖ *What happened to Our Democracy?*
- ❖ *Not a stranger Anymore*
- ❖ *The Secrets of Gabriel*

Coming soon!!!

- ❖ The Return of the Oracle (Unequally Yoking Part two)
- ❖ *The Price of the Arab Revolution*
- ❖ *The covenant Breakers*
- ❖ *The Mischievous widow*
- ❖ *You have my memories*

Order copies of this author's books directly from

www.kpcbooks.com

Or

www.Ziifix.com

ZENTS SOWUNMI

A NOVEL

UNEQUALLY

YOKING

KORLOKI

AN IMPRINT OF KORLOKI PUBLISHERS INC

A

KORLOKI

BOOK

Even when I lose,

I know I am still winning

Because I have you

John Legend

APPRECIATION

My thanks to many of my readers and those who inspired me to keep on writing and those who supported this book when it first came out as a series of ten free online chapters on Social Media?

I am grateful to Ms. Adebisi Osoba in London, the United Kingdom, and Ms. Demetra Bell in El Paso Texas in the state of Texas both of them kept me busy with words of encouragement to finish the book on time, Ms. John a Nurse with Brooklyn Center for Rehab and Nursing who first read this book when it was in the formative stage.

Also, glad to have the support of Mr. Gladstone Adams and Della Faye in Texas, Dauda Abubakar in Abuja the Federal Capital of Nigeria, and many more.

Thanks to you all.

Zents Sowunmi

07/28/2018

UNKNOWN

We have been through so much, we have gotten a lot closer, which I think naturally happens with raising a family together you have history, you have memories.

All your memories are based on time together, so you do not have separate experiences. You have this person you live with who really knows you and you know them so well.

You are not lovers or boyfriends and girlfriends as much as you are a family.

Angolina Joli

MEMPHIS, TN

• •

NOVEMBER 1987

CHAPTER

1

Pastor PJ was almost in tears when he spoke at the funeral service of Tina Wilson, one of his Church members, who died of ovarian cancer, a terminal disease, at the age of 40 years.

The Pastor reminded the congregation of how Tina gave it all to the Church, her time and all her energies, he asked the congregation to emulate the good work of the departed member, and he informed the Church, the South room prayer place would be named after Tina Wilson.

Most of the ladies agreed, some rolled their eyes as if the Pastor went too far to name a prayer place of all places in the sanctuary after Tina, but the men felt the Pastor was right.

And why would they not agree?

All the Church members cried profusely, except her ex-husband John in the front seat who cursed and hissed, and breathed heavily, he had a pitilessly face, and at the end of the service he went to whisper something into the ears of the Pastors, what was it?

Tina was indeed an incredibly beautiful lady; she was tall, and elegant, and with infectious smiles that could disarm a soldier even in the most difficult area of Iraqi fundamentalist dangerous war zones.

Call her the stallion of beauty, you could be right, she gave her life to the Lord, she served the Pinnacle Pentecostal Church with all her time and energies, all the days of the week, she devoted to the Church, on Sunday, she led the Choir, with her melodious voice which reminded congregations of the sexy voice of American Superstar Beyoncé, on Tuesday, it was the time for digging deep prayer time, she was the most active member of the group.

Even the Lord knows it, she could pray, she knew all the verses of the Bible to support all her prayer points, on Friday nights, she assisted the Pastor, to organize the night vigil, and by the time she got home early on Saturday, she was ready for the House fellowship in the evenings, that was the weekly programs of Tina, the most beautiful Lady in the City of Memphis in the State of Tennessee in the United States of America.

Tina had three things that could mesmerize any man, her beautiful long legs, when she walked, she moved and stretched them like a cat and it affected the movement of her butts, with a tiny visible movement as if they were gliding under her gown, that little movement of her butts became one of the weaknesses of most men, if not all the men in the Church they fantasized as if they wanted her now, not even in future and she knew it herself, with a huge smile on her face all the time, and her lips that were full like that popular American singer Donna Sommer who did super hit "winter melody song" in the seventies, Tina's eyes were very tempting enough to undress most men.

However, she was also a single mother, who divorced her husband, John, for reasons she never shared with her trusted friends, all they could think of, was how she changed and devoted all her time to the Church and it became a concern for all her social and childhood friends that relocated with her from New York to live in the City Memphis in the eighties.

The Big Apple City, New York had become too much of a problem for all the young ladies of her age, no serious men for them, none of them was lucky enough to have more than one or two outings before the relationship ended.

At first, they thought if they slept with the men in their lives on their first night, it would lead to a serious relationship, but that did not work out well either and they ended being used, in their hearts, they were lonely and unfulfilling. Men are users, at least, that was the way they all saw it. Six of them felt they have had enough would rather be angels in the state of Virginia, than being a one night stand to most men in New York City, because of the nature of their work and too much time with the traffic and mostly with the subway and cost of living, together, the six of them moved out of New York for a new state with prospects for young ladies, that was in the early eighties.

However, after two years, they could not find the State of Virginia different from New York, until they finally relocated to the City of Memphis, in the State of Tennessee, the home of Elvis, and other Civil rights movement leaders of the sixties, most Americans called Memphis the Music City or so, but it was fine with them, the City met all their expectations. It was quiet and lay back unlike fast tempo New York or any city in the state of Virginia.

Tina Wilson found a perfect Apartment on Station Avenue on the outskirt of the City Memphis, on a sixteen-story building, a comfortable and lovely two bedrooms, and two bathrooms, and far-reaching closets, the comfort of it was different from the space-challenged City of New York.

From the living room through her window, she could see the sky, the stars, and also from her bedroom window she could view or smell the beauty of Mississippi, the only river in the City, and she sometimes wondered why they named the river Mississippi. It was heavenly, her dreams and hopes related to the sceneries of her room, and it was the place she felt more comfortable to pray if she wanted to have a quiet time with her Maker.

As fate would also have it, Tina was also the first among the six ladies to find a serious relationship, her dating period with John was quickly translated to marriage because that was what they both wanted. After two years of trying and using the golden seal medication which the Oracle the friend of John recommended for most ladies with a difficult birth.

Tina was finally pregnant; she gave birth to a bouncing baby body. She named him Samuel. He was such a darling to her. She loved him to death, she tainted the kid with affection, but strangely to the surprise of all, as soon as the boy turned two years, Tina filed for divorce from her husband John, thus, she ended the five-year relationship including marriage with John, she failed to give details of what led to the divorce to her friends, and she withdrew more and more to herself and she attended the Church more to the discomforts of all those around her.

"Maybe we should find her a new man," Rocio said, with her Columbian assent.

"You think she was not going to be too picky?" Marie asked.

Each one of her friends came up with names of eligible men around until they were able to zero it to Larry Dribs, a middle-class African American, who migrated from Liberia in the early eighties, they talked about his qualities, he was muscular, about six feet tall, with appealing smiles, hardworking, besides, he was already making six figures in dollars, he could be a perfect match for Tina with her expensive taste for shopping in high-class stores, they thought.

They called it blind dates; however, after Tina met Larry, she told her perplexed friends that the chemistry was not there.

"I did not feel attracted to him." She said.

"Why will you not? He is such a good-looking guy?" Marie quarried.

"I don't just like the way he grabbed his Glass of Beer," She said mulishly.

"What about it?" Rocio asked.

"He displayed no Class with it," Tina said.

"Larry was not a true Christian either, he did not pray before his meal and I noticed he drank his Beer with his entire mustache soaked inside his glass and at one time, he carelessly, drank his beer straight from the bottle outside the glass he had on his table as if he was in a hurry to finish the drinks to honor another date or appointment." She added.

"Ummm," Rocio said.

"I am very skeptical of any man who would drink only Beer instead of wine on a first date. He must be cheap." Tina said with a mischievous smile on her thin lips.

She added more than what the ladies could take, she said she watched Larry closely with the way he selfishly pushed the food into his mouth as if he was not ready to share the meal with anyone.

"When he crushed the fish eyes like a merciless man from the jungle, I was through with him," Tina said with a dry laugher.

"Why would you think like that?" Rocio asked.

"It is a red flag sign in future; he could be mean, if any man could eat the fish eyes on his first date like a grinding machine, it must be a sign that he might lack feelings in future." She said.

"I have never thought of any relationship between the fish eyes and dating," Rocio said with a mischievous smile on her face.

Tina refused to see Larry again or visited any African restaurant again despite several calls from him.

It was over for her.

Persistently, her friends never stopped trying; they found another guy named Ronaldo for Tina, he came from Puerto Rico, he was a former footballer, a Catholic who never missed any of the morning Mass in his Church and he had two boys from his previous marriage, his wife died in a motor accident along Highway 95 South, 20 miles to Washington DC several years ago, as good and as promising his profile was, Tina would not see him.

The Bible says, "Thou shall not unequally Yoke, because the Roman Catholic denomination members to us Pentecostals, that are true *born-again Christian* cannot be true Christians." she said.

"What is the difference?" Mary asked.

"They worship Saint Mary, the mother of Jesus Christ like a God, they take Holy Communion as if it is a regular daily breakfast, they jump when the Pope talk, and they can't be true Christians." She concluded.

That was two years ago, they gave up on her. Somehow, one of the Ladies had dreamt about Tina being pregnant again and when she was told about the dream, she said, she was never going to have another baby.

"Jesus is now my Husband." She said.

Tina devoted more time to the Church, until one day out of nowhere, she asked one of her friends, Mary to accompany her to the abortion Clinic in a small city outside Memphis.

At first, Mary thought Tina had made it up with John, her ex-husband and she was not ready for another Baby since John was frequent in the last year to see his son.

Maybe she got pregnant for him and she was not ready yet, at least that was the impression she gave her as a confidant, and she made her swear never to disclose that abortion process with any of the four ladies.

Mary gave her word on it, but she never stopped wondering who she was responsible for her pregnancy if it was not John.

Tina's death had not been unexpected, the Doctor had given her six months to live after she was diagnosed with Ovarian Cancer, Congestive Heart Failure (CHF), and Cancer of the Lungs, and everyone from far and near came to spend the last few months with her, but as the months towards her death became weeks and days, and the clock ticking, Tina got very heartlessly mean to all, it must be the Chemotherapy treatment they thought, despite everything they all tolerated her annoyances and ugly behavior.

In most cases, Tina could be very irritating, and she would scream at the top of her voice, the pain was too much as cancer continued to spread all over her womb.

She lost her beautiful hair curls to the chemotherapy treatment too, her eyes got sucked deeper into the cavity of her eyes sockets, and fear was written all over her face like prey in the presence of the ferocious eyes of a Lion. Death was coming to her doorstep, she knew it, her friends could see it too, and slowly and painfully she felt every inch of it from the agony of pain to an unending grimace of hopelessness, and every moment of the torturing demise process.

Earlier in the night, she was deeply in pain, she stretched her hands as if she was beckoning to someone after the Oncology Nurse, an immigrant from Ethiopia in Africa had applied another dosage of Morphine into the IV, the most advanced pain medication in the Oncology Department of St Catherine Hospital in Memphis she closed her eyes as if she was relieved of the pain by the early morning of Saturday, the death she feared for six months finally came; she died

Tina died with one of her eyes still opened, just one eye was closed, it must be a sign of something or why not the two eyes the Nurse wondered, in her tribe in Africa among the Bantus it was not a good sign to die with one eye still opened the Bantus called witchcraft syndrome. She called the Doctor and her family to report the patient expired.

On Saturday evening, after the funeral service, Tina was buried in a place not too far from the Church and the mourning was over, the drums stopped beating, the tears dried. Tina was gone; she had to be with the Lord, many in the Church thought.

Or where else could she be?

What a born-again Christian who gave everything to the Lord, her time and all her energies, that was two months ago. Until John her ex-husband, the father of her only son Samuel, received a notification letter from the City of Memphis and Butterfly Apartment Manager to clean up Tina's apartment and to remove all her kinds of stuff, otherwise, it would be given to the Goodwill or Salvation Army.

Somehow, when you die, you can no longer keep secrets, whatever you hide from the world or the people very close to you will be unprotected from the eyes of those you were hiding it from, in the first place.

What did John find out?

CHAPTER

2

𝕵ohn could still recollect what the Oracle said several years ago when they first met, he said when you die, you can't keep any secret anymore, the very things you jealously kept hidden from the world, from friends and your enemies will be left unprotected, the world would see you for who you were, it could be shameless, and it could be honorable, whatever it was, you will never be around to defend or argue your case, the verdict of history will chase you forever, in most cases, what people kept as a secret before they die were usually the dirty kinds of stuff, what Tina had in her secret closet was not only ugly, it was stinking.

John had a problem, inside him he listened too much to a whispering sprit, the tiny voice that could communicate with him alone, regularly, it often told him what to do, and whatnot, however, in Tina's Apartment the whispering spirit was silent, and John was worried, with the level of emotions in the sermon the Pastor hipped on his late ex-wife, he needed to hear the whispering desperately.

John was even touched by the comment of an old lady who sat next to him in the Church, she whispered to her friend on the other side, in a husky voice that the Pastor spoke like a man who slept with Tina before, not just one time but several times, it was almost the same thing he had whispered into the ears of the Pastor after the sermon.

"She must be more than just a good member of your Church Pastor." He had said, in a voice that sounded more like a statement of fact after the service and he was surprised by the look on the face of the Pastor.

The first Saturday, after John received the notification from the Butterfly Apartment Manager and the City of Memphis to remove Tina's stuff from the Apartment, John went through all her kinds of stuff one by one. He read all her papers page by page, but so far, there was nothing to show there was anything amorous between his late ex-wife and any other person, not even a remote slightest link to anyone, if there was, it was indeed a well-kept secret. And Tina did a good job of it, he thought.

John packed everything back in the cases and he was about to move the purple jacket he gave her ten years ago when he found a key holder with PJ engraved on it. PJ was the nickname for the Pastor. John almost dismissed any stupid notion that first came to his mind until the same whispering spirit told him to tarry over his discovery.

"This could be it." The voice told him.

"Really?" He said to himself as if he was having a conversation with the whispering spirit.

John picked the key holder up, for about five minutes or so, he kept looking at it, as if it would talk to him, or something, but after five minutes or so, he gave it up, he put the key holder back into the jacket, he felt he had had enough, the movers would have to take care of the rest, he stood up and walked towards the door and just as he was about to get out of the apartment, he noticed a little Mickey Mouse on the dining table, it was busy eating the crumbs from the table, he literarily pulled the table sideways as if to distract the mouse.

John hated the mouse in any form, no matter how tiny the mouse could be. As soon as he got closer to the table, it jumped, it leaped and ran behind the refrigerator, he made effort to chase it, and he pulled and rolled the big refrigerator out. He looked behind the Refrigerator if he could see the mouse.

John found himself starring at a little brown pocketbook that was skillfully placed behind the refrigerator. He was surprised, he grabbed the pocketbook. He walked back into the living room, he sat on the edge of the sofa as he thought of what could be in the pocketbook and the reason why Tina kept it behind the refrigerator, and just as he sat down the voice kept telling him "this is" the key to all his inscrutability.

John unzipped the bag with an unsteady hand, and it opened; there was a pack of three CDs and some medical records. Why will Tina keep a bag behind the refrigerator? Could it be the source of all his suspicions? He thought. It must be, or what else could it be! He assured himself and still hoping he could be wrong. The voice echoed in his head "keep digging"

He believed the voice now.

John deliberated within himself if he should read the medical records or not, at least a dead Tina would no longer need the document, he thought, he will not be running against HIPPA regulation as his left hand was shaking, he loved Tina from the first day they met, till they parted ways, he had slept with lots of women in his life, but none gave him the pleasure like her, he had explored and searched with the hope he would find someone else but she was like a virus in his vein.

Even in death, Tina was all over his emotions and feelings, her love had robbed him of all his memories, her smiles, her teeth and the way she made love to him could never be duplicated by any woman, she was the tigress in the bedroom, always in charge of everything.

What a Lady of grace? He never stopped thinking.

John reminisced on how he came to Memphis and how he was allured to the Pinnacle Pentecostal Church, six months after he had left the City of San Antonio in Texas for the City of Memphis in Tennessee because of his promising new job.

"You need to fellowship with the brothers." He was told by one of his colleagues at work. And that was how he got his invitation to attend Pinnacle International mission located on Greenville Avenue of the City.

The Church program had started with melodious songs from the hyperactive choirs, they danced, they clapped and it kept the Congregation going and when it was time for the announcement, one of the presiding pastors in the church asked new members or visitors to stand up for recognition, as it was the practice in most Pentecostal Churches in the South.

John donned one of his best suits on that Sunday, and it was his first-time service with the Pinnacle Church, he had his pure leather Gucci shoe on an Italian snake leather belt, believe it or not, John loved himself when he looked at the mirror before he came to the Church service that day, sometimes, he would say to himself.

"You are a good-looking brother." He knew he was special, and something else to behold for the single ladies.

Yes, he was good-looking with a thin pencil lined mustache, and see-through eyeglasses that will make any woman steal more than just a glance at him. He cut his hair low every week, he never failed to apply his cologne and deodorant, he smells good all the time and most women placed him on top of their list.

When John stood up along with few others to be acknowledged, he became the most sorts after in the Church by all the singles, he was more like a basketball superstar because he introduced himself to the Congregation that he was single, it was the magic word for all the single ladies who were actively looking, everyone wanted a piece of him.

Tina was one of the ladies in charge of introducing new members to the procedures of the Church but on that day, she was on another assignment for the Pastor.

John was standing by the door when he saw Tina for the first time, as she walked to the altar to get the Holy Communion, her beauty mesmerized his faith, he noticed the slight movement of her butts, his mouth was wide open and he knew immediately she would be his woman, but how could anyone talk to Lady in the house of God in the presence of all during the Holy Communion process?

He asked himself.

John watched her intensely even more as she opened her mouth to receive the Holy Communion, her tongue was graciously placed on top of her teeth, she closed her eyes, and everything was gracefully done. She stood up gently and she walked down the passage, he followed her with his eyes, and just by divine intervention, her eyes met his, he felt he saw her blinked more than three times, he could not be sure, but he knew he saw something special, she had a slight smile on her lips, he was not born yesterday, he knew the look when a woman wanted a man, he suspected she had the same feelings for him like he did for her.

They called it Chemistry, and whatever the solutions in the chemical mixture were, he intended to explore it further.

When she walked past him to her seat, he could smell her friendly perfume, which was how close and desperate he was to her in the house of God. He immediately lost interest in the Holy Communion himself, he left the line and walked towards her seat, but all the seats around her were all taken, he felt the Lord Jesus of Nazareth would have to understand this daughter of Jezebel would be his own Holy communion that Sunday.

When the service was over, as Tina walked towards her black BMW car neatly packed on the left corner of the lot, John approached her, and as he was about to say something, his mouth was dried, he had never felt like that before. She smiled at him, he saw her teeth, they were white and well arranged, and with dimples on both sides of her checks. It was the most beautiful smile with teeth, he had ever seen in his life. Her smiles took his breath away and his heart was pounding profusely. He felt like a teenager approaching his first love life.

"I noticed your eyes all over me while we were taking the Holy Communion." She said.

It was more like a statement than a question, that even made him more to be dumbfounded, he lost his ability to speak, or why would any lady be the first to start a conversation in any relationship? He asked himself.

She extended her hand to him first, which even surprised him more. He noticed she had no ring on her left hand, her nails were polished black. She could not have grown up in the South may be from the East Coast, he thought. Why?

Only women from the East Coast would paint their nails black or talk to men first not in the South.

John took her hand, it was warm and a little wet, he kissed the back of her hand like the French. He liked the look on her face more. She was smiling.

"You might as well tell me your name if you can still find your voice. I am Tina." She said.

John could not even bring himself to telling her his name he forgot his name. He shook her hand again, it was soft and a little warm, his eyes never left her face for a second, and somehow he looked down a bit towards her chest, and he could see her nipples sumptuously pointing at him. He quickly looked away. It was not until she entered her car and was almost pulling out of the lot before he found his voice.

"I have a name. I am John." He was almost shouting at the top of his voice.

She laughed as she drove off. It was then he remembered he did not have her telephone number except to wait until next Sunday with the hope she would come back.

The waiting was killing becauses her beauty and smiles tortured him throughout the week. He thought of her, at work, he looked around for her face in the grocery stores, and when he was driving around, even at traffic stop signs, he hoped the next car would be hers; any black BMW looked like hers to him.

John could not figure out why a brief encounter in the Church and direct talk with Tina in the parking lot for just two minutes or so could change his life.

It surely did.

Finally, the Sunday service came, John looked his best, he had his best suit on, a light grey, he changed his cologne, he brushed his teeth twice, his tongue was properly cleaned, he knew he had to close this deal; else he would be miserable for the rest of his life. If it was not a deal what else could it be?

He asked himself again and again.

John came to the Church earlier than usual, he had reserved the seat next to him for her or hoping the seat beside her would be empty as soon, but when Tina came in, a little late to the Church, she had a light blue dress on that gave her beauty the fragrance of the moment. He almost called out on her in the presence of all that the next seat to him was for her. She walked her way to the front seat and she gracefully sat down, and she did the sign of Cross.

All the seats around her were taken, all John could see was only the back of her head and it was not how he planned his Sunday in the Church with her, he wanted her next to him.

Throughout the service, John could not remember what the sermon or the verses of the Bible that were used that day, all he was thinking was the woman in the front with her back at him, and he kept on hoping she would at least turn her head briefly to see him, wave at him or something, he felt like having the power to ask the Pastor to fast track the service from two hours to forty minutes.

John was glad when the boring service was finally over. Yes boring, it was the way he saw the service that day.

After the service in the Parking lot, he found his voice, he was the first to talk to her as she was made her way to the car lot.

"Hi, Tina," John said.

"Oh! You found your voice today, was it the miracle the Pastor talked about?" She mocked him.

"You are my miracle, Tina." He said. His voice sounded more like a bedroom voice and he meant every word of it.

"Let us go grab lunch while you can tell about yourself and the miracle I am famished," she said humorously.

"What do you have taste for, Seafood or Mexican food?" John asked eagerly.

"Red Lobster is fine with me." She said.

They dated for six months. She never allowed him to make love to her until they got married, and she told him, her Bible instructed the Christian women to make love to their husbands alone, not boyfriends, so he waited until the night, after the wedding.

The marriage was not elaborate; the crowd could not have been more than forty people. It was the way she wanted it. Immediately they came back from the Church, she had instructed him to take a warm bath, and like a kid who listened to his Mom, he did exactly, what she told him.

The warm water was sprinkling on his head, he was thinking of the future with the woman who would share the rest of her life with him. He recalled the first time he had kissed Tina, her tongue was like a snake, it curled around his mouth, and like a string around his tongue, no woman had ever given him such pleasure in his life, he was thrilled to the last marrow, her touch made his legs weak, and he wanted more and more, and she gave him until he moved to unhook her bra when she stopped him.

"Don't let the Devil tempt us to go beyond kissing darling." She whispered into his ears.

"What was that about the devil?" He thought.

"I hope you would understand." She pleaded.

Who cares, all he wanted was the Devil to tempt him but he knew Tina to be special, she was not like all the ladies he had slept with since he moved to Memphis; take it easy with her, he told himself.

"She is the one, take it easy with her." The tiny voice in his head cautioned him.

"I will wait until you are ready Darling." He replied

That was six months into their relationship, but tonight she was his wife.

"Let the Devil tempt us tonight." John almost shouted it out.

He stepped into the bedroom, his own Tina, the love of his life was waiting, and he had a mischievous smile on his face, as he walked towards her, and tonight would be the night, our night. He said to himself.

It was a good night for them, they started slowly, as they kissed and kissed, she found him to be a tidy guy, he caressed her breast with the tip of his tongue until she was finally ready for him.

The sound of Etta James's song *"At last my love has come along"* was going on in the background, he found himself humming the song himself when the lyric said *"my lonely days are over"* Tina was completely naked, except for her underwear, this time, she made no effort to stop him when he attempted to yank it off with his left hand, she did not even quote any of the King James verses of the Bible. If she wanted anything from the Holy Book tonight, it must be the forbidden fruits.

"I love you John with all my heart." She said.

"You are all my love." He told her.

John could see from the urgency and movement of her sumptuous lips, tonight she was ready to be the woman for him the woman to complete his life.

John with his mouth almost glued to hers, he skillfully rolled down her underwear, gently to her smooth knees, down further to her ankle, he touched her nose with the tip of his tongue, he blew a little air into her ears, she trembled like someone in the cold weather of Alaska, he felt the goose of her skin, they were like silky carpet, he knew she was ready for him, he moved inside her and she mourned not because he was too big for her. She was in the heavens of love for the man she planned to live the rest of her life with.

Tina was not a virgin, but she was not a loose lady, she was tight, she was more than he had expected. He made love to her several times and the more he pounded her, the more she wanted him more, the more he gave her. She was wild, her tempo was erotic, and her movement was more like she was following the script of a song until he was exhausted.

John told himself the waiting was worth it like Michael Jackson said in the new song in the background; *she was rocking his world with the way she moved and how she gave it to him.*

John worked so hard to keep his marriage; he lost most of his childhood friends because Tina said so. She was the boss in the relationship. She picked his new friends for him, but his job as traveling medical personnel took him out of the town three days a week, those days Tina was in the Church.

The first five years of the marriage did not produce babies; they took all the supplements from folic acid and Vitamin E to improve the fertility still nothing came until John met the Oracle, who introduced him to the Goldenseal medication.

At first, Tina would not use the medication, she talked about waiting on the Lord's time, and she quoted the Bible and talked about Sarah who was very old before she conceived, until John jokingly told her he did not plan to compete with Abraham in the baby creation process.

Finally, she took the medication from the Oracle, and six months later she conceived, when the baby boy came, she named him Samuel and the whole Church came for the Christening of the boy. Pastor PJ was the Godfather of the only baby of the marriage.

Two years after the birth of Samuel, it was over. It was how far the marriage lasted. Tina filed for a divorce and John had to move out, and things were never the same anymore. Everything was like yesterday; it was a nasty memory for John.

Looking back at all those years now in her apartment John pulled out a stick of cigarette from the pack of Newport menthols from his pocket, he looked at the neatly packed cigarette box, and he deliberated on it and wondered why his own life was not well arranged like the pack of the cigarettes in his hand. He lighted the cigarette and in between his thick lips, he dragged the smoke down his lungs, and it was smooth and relaxing.

"Thank God for Philips Morris," he told himself. "

What is better than a cigarette when things are not working well?" he told himself.

"Nothing!" He said aloud as if answering the question himself.

John sat down, he pushed in one of the three CD's he had found in the pocketbook behind the refrigerator into the CD player, he could not believe what he saw.

What did he see?

CHAPTER

3

𝔍ohn rested his head on the couch; he thought of his life with Tina, and the future of his son Samuel, he pressed down the silver button on the remote control, the picture came up on the 52 inches Philips television flat screen, he had given her a few years ago.

Tina had wanted the Television for their son's birthday; it was all she said before he ran out like a chicken without head to Best Buy stores to purchase it. If that would make her happy and with the hope, the marriage will be fixed, he was ready to do anything for her.

On the television screen, the picture came up. The love of his life Tina, in her beauty, was in a bikini that exposed her beautiful legs that drove him crazy. She was not alone. She was with seven other beautiful women, some of them he had seen in the Church before they were all in their sexually aroused dressed pattern; they stood by the swimming pool with lots of men, most of them donned in suits like Wall Street executives.

John could pick up some of the faces; they were the power brokers of the City of Memphis, from the current and past Mayors, Chief of Police, legislators and later Pastor PJ walked in with Gina, his charming wife to meet with the group that would propel the Church to a 25,000 member's capacity if the plans could be followed.

All the women behaved more like marketers, they were to sexually escort the politicians to donate more than tithes to the Church, besides, they were to do all they could to empty the wallets of the power brokers in the City and the

State, the Church in return would tailor the service and programs to ensure all the affected donors were in the good book of the society.

It was the program Tina coordinated for the Pastor and the Church, they were all signing some papers and what was in it would be known in the future.

At first, John could not understand if he was watching a movie about the love of his life Tina. He often referred to her as his Angel. He saw the Mickey Mouse again, this time; he did not chase it, why would he chase his God-sent angel?

Maybe he should be grateful to the little mickey mouse which made him see the other side of his unprotected life, the mickey mouse moved to the kitchen, he followed it with his eyes, what a beautiful little creature, with a shining tail, glittering eyes, and fast-moving lips, not unmindful of its environment, he wondered, if the little mickey ever slept at all, he reached for his cigarette again, he stamped the pack on his left-hand palm, he looked at the pack of Newport cigarette, as if it was all the only friend he had now, and he was about to burn the friend, he lighted the cigarette, he drew the smoke straight to his lungs and felt relieved, it does not matter again, he told himself.

All the eight years of thinking of how and why his marriage collapsed came to a let go situation for him, somehow, he was curious, he wanted to see the end of the movie or what could it be? But what he saw was more than he bargained for.

He pushed in the second CD.

Tina was naked on the bed, in what could pass for a guest house; she was reading a playboy Magazine until the doorbell rang. He saw how she jumped like a kid expecting candies from the parent. She ran to the door as if she was expecting the caller for months, she did not even bother to put on her clothes, she was completely naked like a mermaid.

As he looked at her now on the screen, he knew how and why she stole his heart. She had the best body in the South to him, and looking at her on the television screen, he felt like joining her in the room, he felt a movement with his manhood as the door opened and Gina, the first lady of the Church, the wife of Pastor PJ came in, they hugged each other, and within seconds, the Pastor's wife too like Tina was naked too, their breast were tantalizing, they were kissing each other with all the passion anyone could imagine, and also touching all their anatomical private parts.

It was like a lion attacking a helpless prey in the jungle, both women wanted each other like the bees wanted the honey, more like a river needed the ocean, and it was like they would never have enough of each other.

John had often thought his wife was the Tiger in his relationship, but here, the two women were, they kissed all the parts of their bodies, and the First Lady of the Church reached for her bag, she brought out adult toys for sex, and what could be taken as marijuana, they smoked and made love to each other, with the sex toys.

Somehow, John found tears coming out of his left eye only. Tina the woman he loved unconditionally with all his heart, despite everything, was also a Lesbian.

John cleared his throat; he needed a drink by now as his head was pounding. He also needed the Aspirin for it, he kept on dragging the smoke harder into his lungs but somehow, he found himself aroused and was wondering, what these daughters of Jezebel were going to do next.

The doorbell rang, they made no effort to open it, but whoever it was had his key and the door was pushed open. Surprisingly, Pastor PJ came in, he made straight for the bedroom. John sat up quickly at the edge of the chair, he wanted to know what the Pastor was going to do; sadly, the light went off, because Tina never paid the light bill in her last few months in the hospital.

It was difficult to remove the CD; he unplugged the whole CD player, he placed the player and cord in his bag, he was about to get out of the Apartment when he saw the mickey mouse again, he was grateful to the little mickey, which led him to the discovery, he closed the door gently behind him, and walked to his car, his legs were weak, his head was still pounding, he was a little dizzy, but he was still able to drive his car around the city, for about 30 minutes, just to cool off and he was thinking of what to do and what would be in the rest of the last of the three CDs he found.

John found a parking space almost a block from his apartment, He packed the car and walked towards his building, the breeze made his head a little lighter, he kept on walking, he walked around the block twice just to feel the cool air on his pounding head, and it reduced the tension on him.

He lived on the third floor, he climbed the stairs instead of the elevator, he needed the exercise and he ran the stairs, like a man chasing the last few steps of his life until he got to the door of his apartment, the doorknob had a note clipped to it, and it was from the Oracle. It says before you do anything stupid see me, do not even open the door"

The note advised.

Did John open the door to his apartment, or he went straight to see the Oracle?

CHAPTER

4

𝕿wo days after Tina was buried, Pastor Jackson, fondly called PJ by his flocks got a call from Andrew Peterson, the retired Mayor for the City of Memphis who was also the Chairman Board of trustees to the Church; he wanted an urgent meeting with him that evening.

PJ contemplated on what the Old man wanted, that could not be discussed on the telephone, everything appeared to be under control, the Church was growing, all the investments of the mission in the Banks and other places were doing just fine, membership was growing and the worshipers were sending in their tithes regularly with a broad smile on their faces. In the next two years, Pinnacle International Services will hit the 25,000-membership target.

"What could be wrong?" He asked himself.

PJ loved the system the Church had with the First Nation Bank which Andrew Peterson introduced to the Church two years ago. It made it easier for members to pay their tithes and donations with the credit cards, it was a boom to the mission, the revenue went up more than 250 %, the Church should be moving to the 100 acres site outside Memphis and members were coming up with different programs to expand the Church and its international outreach ministries.

PJ reminisced how he grew up on the East side of Brooklyn New York, somewhere on Fountain Avenue close to Euclid in the tough Eastside of New York. It was rough, his family came from a very poor background as immigrants from the Dominican Republic, they could only live in the basement of a building his parent rented from a Landlady he knew as

Mrs. Smith who also migrated from Jamaica in the early sixties, people practically lived on the streets in the East Side of Brooklyn, they smoked weeds freely and talked very loudly, with the blasting music on both sides of the streets.

As a teenager, PJ would watch the "C" train from the Subway and would sometimes be tempted to run away, when he grew up more, he told himself, if he was able to leave Brooklyn New York, he was never going to set his foot on the East Side of the City again.

That was his dream then.

The Brooklyn Heights High School he attended contained lots of gangs, they all experimented with cracks and marijuana, sometimes with cocaine, it was fashionable to be high on drugs then, he was glad, when his Uncle David from the City of Durham, in the State of North Carolina, came to get him and his brother Patrick after his High School Diploma which he managed to pass, he was an average student, until he got enrolled into the Community college in Durham, he never placed all his energies into academics, when he finally decided to be a Pastor as a career, and he knew he was not going to be just an ordinary Pastor, he would be known all over the country even beyond and he knew one day, he would sit on the Oprah Winfield Show in Chicago or Larry King on CNN, those were his dreams to sit on the same high table with TD Jakes of Dallas Texas

PJ had seen a lot of Oral Roberts Television programs and his worldwide ministries and he hoped to be greater than that in his career and nothing was going to stop him.

Nothing!

That was fifteen years ago, he had matured in his ministry, he knew the rope of the business, the politics behind the growth of the Church, and to invest and save for the rainy day, his association with the politicians had shown him what he could do.

PJ marriage to Gina was doing just fine, it was strictly for business, they did a lot of unspeakable things in the bedroom, the more he tried to please her, the more she wanted, until he realized, she needed more than a partner to keep her sexual needs in control, one thing and the other led to the inclusion of other unspeakable events in their relationship, whatever she wanted she got it, otherwise, she could rock his boat and that he could not afford.

Why did the Chairman ask him for a meeting in his house instead of the usual monthly meeting in the Church premises or the Hilton Hotel they both loved?

He was worried.

PJ knew his financial records were okay. He thought. He knew no one including his wife, Gina would ever notice his secret accounts in the Cayman Islands or the secret businesses, he had outside the country, his brother Patrick, who was never a member of the Church coordinated his sharp practices for him and he lived in the Cayman Islands outside the country far away from the law, in a country the United States of America had no extradition treaty with.

"You need to prepare for the raining day." Patrick had told him, as soon as he was appointed the Pastor for the Pinnacle International Gospel in Memphis, Tennessee.

At the beginning of his first year in office as the pastor of the Church, he was naïve; he reported all incomes and donations. He was too much of plain Jane and trustworthy until his brother had a meeting with him, he coached him, on how to be a successful pastor and a businessman at the same time, there should never be a separation between the two; he could remember what Patrick said.

"You have to combine your ministry with some of the most important strategies in life, Pastor and Businessman, smile often, dress well, and keep a positive attitude, which was all you need to be a good pastor." He said.

"What then is the next step?" PJ asked.

"When you add preaching prosperity to it, thousands of dollars will role in from gullible members, to be a millionaire, you have to do beyond the ordinary, expand your horizon, move beyond the conventions of four P's of marketing, Price, Promotion, products, placement, add the two unmentioned P's to it, power and politics, that was how the millions would role in, not through the Church but from powerful politicians and those seeking favors." He said.

Patrick was right; PJ followed his brother's advice like a student who followed all the principles of the law of gravity from his science teacher or the of Isaac Newton.

Patrick had always been his coach, his mentor, and his protector right from their ugly East side of Brooklyn New York, he knew people, particularly those who could do ugly jobs for him if he had to straighten things out. Out of instinct, before PJ left to see the Chairman, he placed a call to his brother, who gave him the go-ahead.

PJ sat for a few minutes in his White-colored 450 E Class Mercedes Benz 2009 model. He prayed. He did the sign of the cross like the Roman Catholics, it was a habit he picked up in New York, and sometimes he often had to remind himself he was not a Catholic Priest who could ask for confession from his Pentecostal members.

It was a thirty minutes' drive from the mission house to the Chairman's residence, it was almost a year ago, since he visited the House of the Chairman, on the Southside of the City.

PJ noticed the property had been repainted, from the creamy color it had in the past to Whitestone dust, the gate had also been redecorated, it had marble dust he was thinking of his mansion in St Lucia, maybe, he should change the gate to something like this one.

He thought!

PJ rang the doorbell, the Butler, a Black man from Jamaica came to usher him in. He gave PJ a familiar look and he also asked about his family along with other unnecessary social questions. He was not even thinking if he was giving the Butler the right answers to all his questions, his mind was on the unscheduled meeting the Butler took him straight to the Study room.

PJ was astonished, to see all the seven other members of the Board of Trustees in the library room. They were all seated and waiting for him; somehow, he did not trust the mischievous smiles on their faces when he shook their hands.

He smiled back at them, but his smile was more like a grimace with a strained eye and his body language was more like a watchful cat ready to run in case of any surprise.

He was ready.

PJ Straightened up his necktie, he removed his jacket, he picked the seat remarkably close to the door, which gave him an advantage on the movement and body languages of all those in the room. He was waiting, for the next move from them but the Chairman was still upstairs, like the rest of the trustee, he too waited.

What happened next?

CHAPTER

5

ℜetired Mayor of Memphis Andrew Peterson was the Chairman Board of the Trustee to the Pinnacle International Gospel Services. He was literarily a short man; he lost his wife several years ago in a motor accident on Highway 35 around the City of Waco Texas.

He was stoutly built, his eyes were bigger than usual with an expanded nose, and all his smiles stayed only on his lips, nothing on his greenish eyes like the Cobra, it never exposed his inner self, he was indeed a ruthless businessman using the Church to cover up his dirty linens, and whatever he lacked in his height, he had it in his third legs, very huge manhood, almost a foot long, his penis must be the longest in the City.

It was rumored.

Andrew's manhood was his only weapon on women, he called it a weapon of mass submission, he loved women, but within a parameter of ages, of 35-42 years, usually all his pickups were single ladies in the Church or those who came to the Church more than usual because of simple marital problems at home, only one night was all he asked from any lady, particularly, those who claimed to have separated from their spouses before they all signed away their divorce decrees.

Andrew loved to see his women morn and cry under him, no woman had been able to play the funny fake sex game with him, he knew the rope and the system of sex, and how to pound and pound and it was the cry of pain on the faces of his victims that gave him satisfaction.

However, Tina was different, apart from the sex she gave him once a month, with all her sex toys, the oil, the massaging, and uncontrollable domination in the room with unending feelings that made him ask for more and more. She added spices to her styles better than the rest of all the ladies in the Church. She knew the game better than anyone he ever met.

Tina made him sign a five-page document, and the sex was too much and too good for him to read the whole pages. Unknown to him, he was signing away his future he jealously protected in his years as a public service and three times elected Mayor for the City of Memphis.

Tina's death was a big blow to all the arrangement in place however, Mayor Andrew, got his memory back from her spell, he had called other trustees and they all confessed they too signed a document with all the other eight ladies, more like the recruiters, for the work of Jezebel, none of them, could lay claim to the details of what it contained and maybe the Pastor would have a clue, it was the reason for the meeting and how to move forward. He could not ask for the meeting to take place in Church premises because Christ Jesus may be too close to understand the separation of business from Church.

Andrew Peterson walked into his Study room, all the trustees were all seated, and he noticed none of them touched the coffee and several drinks on the table. Despite the air condition at almost 65 degrees, he could see they all looked as if they needed all the airs in the State of Tennessee.

Who wouldn't be? He asked himself.

PJ could imagine if the Press and FBI should get hold of just 10% of what the Church was doing with the money, and sharp practices behind the holy place, they may be out of circulation for a long time, as for him, he was not ready to go to jail because all the victims of his three-term as Mayor of Memphis were still serving terms in jail due his hash laws against Child molesters they will have a good time with him in jail if ever he was found guilty of any crime, no matter how small.

Three days ago, he had received a tip or a call from Gabriel Wagman who was his mate in the High School, who worked for the government in Washington DC, those guys were funny and scary, they would never call it FBI, each time he called by way of social call; but the last call was different, he just asked how was the Tina doing?

Andrew's throat dried with that question from an FBI agent, it was not just a call, and he knew Gabriel Wagman was giving him a hint or something more like a file was already opened on his business, and it was why he had to tighten the loose end.

Mayor Andrew Peterson sat at the head of the table; he opened the meeting without the usual prayers from the Pastor. He went straight to the business on hand, and with a very direct question.

It made PJ uncomfortable.

"PJ with the death of Tina, the Board would like to ask if you still have access to any document from her, particularly the August 8th document which we all signed years ago, "He said.

PJ cleared his throat; he had expected more than what he got from the Chairman of the Board of Trustees...

"Yes, I have the folder here." He said.

All the members were relieved, they reached for their untouched drinks and coffee for the first time, PJ placed his briefcase on the table, and like hungry kids, they all wanted to know what they all signed years ago.

PJ brought out the folder marked Madame Tina from his briefcase, he placed it on the table, it was almost half an inch thick, it had all the names, fingerprints, and photos of each member of the Board, and all document were the same, in which they all promised to work for the glory of the Church and members alone, nothing secret, just plain Jane document with no strings of any attachment.

Each member reviewed the documents, again and again, page by page they were relieved until the Chairmen noticed the sixth page of the document was missing, they all thought all along they signed five pages what happened?

"What happened to the missing document?" They asked the Pastor.

PJ noticed the missing page for the first time himself after a lot of brainstorming. The Board resolved to search Tina's old Apartment, her secret deposit account if they could lay their hands on anything incriminating to the Church. It was then, like a flashlight, the message John the ex-husband of Tina whispered to his ear during the sermon made him uncomfortable.

"You can't fool the Lord." He had said.

The Board of Trustees will re-convey for another meeting next week, to take stocks of all the activities of the Church, somehow, Mayor Andrew Peterson informed the Board that will be his last year as the Chairman. The venue for the next meeting would be conveyed to members solely by the Chairman, and the meeting was adjourned.

PJ could not bring himself to listen to the CD Gospel in his car on the way home. Maybe, he would not be able to have a seat on Oprah Winfield show in Chicago or Larry King on CNN, if everything; he worked for all his life got blown off in his face like a pack of cards. He still could recall the last time he went to preach to the inmates in his county jail, they looked sexually deprived like castrated dogs, no wonder homosexuals were all they practiced in the county jails.

"I don't want to go to jail." He said, almost loudly to himself.

PJ opened his car's glove compartment, to check his two international passports, America and the Dominican Republic, the country of his parent, with the Visas to the Cayman Islands on then, they were all still valid, and he could recollect what his brother told him if he ever had any problem with the law.

"Just make it to the border town of El Paso in Texas, drop your car with any gas station walk across the downtown to Juarez, the border town with the country of Mexico, and I would take over the rest of for you." Patrick had promised.

PJ gently placed the two passports in the side pocket of his suit; he packed his car in front of the mission house.

He walked in.

What did he see?

CHAPTER
6

Gina in her forties was still ravishingly beautiful as the first lady of the Pinnacle International Gospel Services she took care of her beauty. She was the lady with an unending appetite for sex, by the end of the first year as the wife of the new Pastor; she had slept with all the members of the Board of trustees.

Gina noticed most of the men were sexually weak because none of them was strong enough to meet her of demand and drive except for Andrew Peterson the Chairman Board of Trustees. She wondered why he could not settle down with a woman after the death of his wife in a road accident in Waco Texas, he had everything a woman could want, the drive and the money.

Gina could still remember vividly, the manner and the style of the Chairman Mayor Andrew Peterson when he introduced himself to her after she did a melodious song for the Church.

"You surprised me with your heart thrilling voice." He said.

Andrew's voice was softer like the breeze from the ocean; it affected her skin. Gina's heart was beating amazingly fast, as she took the hand, he extended to her, and it was warmer than usual. She had a charm on most men only a blink from her could seduce any man; it was what she did to the Mayor.

She blinked at him.

"Why did you say that?" She said in a low sexy bedroom voice herself.

"I never thought you could captivate the minds of the audience in such a way." He added.

Andrew parted the back of her hands on both sides as if he was caressing it. She felt something in his touch all over her body, more like the current of electricity and inside her; almost as if they were communicating sexually, she knew instantly, she was going to sleep him, but when?

She blinked her eyes again.

It was less than two months before it finally happened, the phone rang, and the caller wanted to speak to her husband. PJ was not around, it was Mayor Andrew Peterson; they talked as if they knew each other more than the occasional Church activities, before she knew what was going, she was on her way to his house.

When Gina returned home after the first evening with Mayor Andrew Peterson, she had thought of parting away with her husband. Andrew was the best in her life, he knew how to please a woman, he was patient, slow, and very enduring, unlike PJ her husband full of mouth.

She wondered why Mayor Andrew Peterson never wanted to settle down, with another woman after the death of his wife, he had cleverly chipped it in on her on their second nights together, and that marriage was way out of the equation for him.

Gina's marriage to PJ had been rocky, he had no drive, his manhood was little, she wondered if he knew how unhappy she was each time he made love to her. She was getting tired of faking an orgasm, and in most cases, she would be chewing gum while the Pastor would be haplessly pounding her.

It was very disgusting.

Gina had also given up on men as soon as she knew Mayor Andrew Peterson was never going to be within her reach. It was why she started swinging both ways. She went for the single ladies in the Church and outside the mission; recently, she had stopped sleeping with women outside the Church. It could be dangerous, she thought. PJ could no longer meet up with her sexual needs; she kept a folder on him like a tag to keep her position in the family.

As a form of security Gina recorded her conversations with all the men she slept with, and she also kept them in a safe deposit far away in South Padre Island in the South of Texas; it was the trick she got from her mother, who slept with all the men in their neighborhood. When she died, most of the men that came to her funeral had at one time or the other get a piece of her.

Gina's father died of a heart attack two years after her mother died of lung cancer. He was strong and healthy until he stormed into the secret document of his late wife, her conversations with all the men some of them were his best friends and business associates, and recorded videos of all her inequities.

Gina's father was found dead with his mouth wide open by the kitchen table with all the documents spread out on the floor. When Gina saw the papers herself with all the dirty linens of her mother, she read them all, page by page, and took note of some of the mastery of the game of adultery from her. She, however, destroyed everything and she challenged herself to be smarter than her mother. She kept her document in a secret deposit account in South Padre in South Texas far away from the eyes of her almost impotent husband.

However, as soon as she became bisexual, she found Tina to be the best, of all. They went into partnership with many crimes in addition to sleeping around; they focused more on the revenue which the Church was generating monthly. She planted a computer chip into the system that drew seven cents per dollar from any amount paid through the credit card system.

Every month, both were sharing from the secret account that was generating over $150,000 and within two years, both of them had millions of dollars from all the sharp practices in their secret accounts, the bulk of the fund went to an account in South Dakota before a programed system would split it into 50 percent each to their accounts outside the country.

It was not enough; the sixth missing document on the papers the Board of Trustee signed contained all the bank accounts and secret codes of all the investments of the sex-starved directors, which alone, generated an average of $200,000 every quarter. It was the fund she distributed among the nine ladies that slept with the Board of a trustee from time to time, her fear was prominent, the women were getting older, and the men were already looking at the younger ladies to the discomfort of the group. And very soon she would have to address this issue of gradual replacement.

Tina's death was a big blow to the group, and a replacement was not easily found, she was the Director of the program with lots of innovations. Gina was restless and uninitiated, without Tina, who had the code to most of the document that could send all the men in the Church to jail for a long time, she was helpless.

Gina often wondered how most of the men could be porous and stupid enough to have signed away their careers, as soon as they saw a lady's thigh, and breast, some of them would crawl, or be allowed to be tied like a dog to bed pole.

Gina had told the ladies to get the photographs of the men in their stupid positions if they wanted a bonus at the end of the months, and they all did. In other words, Tina was the planner, while Gina executed the programs from the corporate level.

Gina was still in her world thinking of the future without Tina when her husband PJ walked in, he looked dejected and worried, he greeted her casually, he did not kiss her, and he went to his table, and what could he be looking for?

She wondered.

She followed him with her eyes, in the next five hours it will be time for the Sunday service, it does not look as if he was ready with the Sermon to preach to almost 12,000 members that may likely be in the Church.

PJ sat down on the leather couch. Gina pitied him, she walked to him, she placed her hands on his shoulder, and she drew him closer and planted a kiss on his lips.

"Baby, how was your day? She asked.

"Just fine," He said.

But PJ was thinking of the missing document. He did not even kiss her back.

"Will you care to join me in the Bedroom I have something for you tonight?" She said seductively.

"Ummm. Okay, love." He said.

PJ watched Gina as she went straight to the bedroom. He was worried. He knew he needed a powerful sermon to keep the Church vibrant; they loved him when he preached and stretched more on the imperfections of Apostle Peter in Holy Books.

Any sermon on Peter the Apostle made the whole congregations to feel the spirit of the Lord in them, some will cry, some will blame themselves more for all the sins they committed, seen and unseen sins, the single ladies would hate their boyfriends more, most of the married women would go home to deny their husband sex because their body was the temple, a temple to be kept away from the sins of Eve. It was the message he talked all the time or what could the body be, if not the Temple of God?

PJ knew the weaknesses of women more than the men in his Church, they attended the programs more than the men, they were too porous and very attentive in the Church than the men, from years he noticed, men slept most of the time, or they who never stopped thinking of the next game of basketball and football, he wondered why those two games were invented at all and even played on Sundays.

During the service he would stress the offering and donations as the only way to heaven, PJ would hammer it more and more, by the time it was time for offerings, they will be too weak to understand, everything was business to him, the checks will be rolling in and he would notice the smiles on faces of the Board of trustees.

If PJ was happy, he was not alone, his wife and group of eight women were equally happy because whatever the process the goodwill out of service was spreading around like the rain to all the stakeholders.

The Sunday service was packed full, somehow, all the members of the Board of trustees were all there, the Choir had elected Ana as the new lead singer for the group after the death of Tina. She was good and all the activities were in place until it was time for the Pastor to deliver his sermon.

PJ Stood up, he thanked the Lord for the day, and the whole Church shouted Hallelujah, the drums and strings of Hawaiian guitar complimented every shout of Hallelujah.

"Let the people of the Lord open the book of John verse 5-6, "He said. They all did and those who could not saw the verses PJ was about to preach from the flat screens all over the walls of the Church.

The sermon was just into three minutes when one of the ushers approached the PJ on the pulpit with a short note, he did not even read it, he placed the note in his pocket, and he kept on with the sermon.

However, two minutes after, the Usher came again and whispered into the left ear of the Pastor, that the sender asked him to inform the Pastor to read the note or he would come to the pulpit to read the content of the note very clearly himself to the Congregation.

PJ opened the note, it was a few lines statement which asked him to stop the service and see the writer outside the Church immediately.

Did he stop the service?

What happened next?

CHAPTER

7

John believed the Oracle more than anyone in the community. He cherished his advice and traditional wisdom which was always unusual in his community. He did not open the door to his apartment; he headed back to his car, he placed the CD player and remaining two CDs and unopened medical document he found in Tina's apartment in his gloves compartment of his car and headed to the Oracle's place in downtown Memphis.

John could still recall how he met the oracle several years ago, it was by divine interventions, they were standing by the Metro station in Chicago, waiting for the next train, the waiting was killing, life was not as good as he had expected when he graduated from the University of Chicago as a Medical Technologist.

And waiting for the train was equally as boring as the marshy and greasy environment and he needed someone to talk to. He noticed the man next to him, had an unusual band on his wrist. It was remarkably close to how his anthropology Instructor, mentioned in one of his scary classes about five years ago.

Professor James had told the class, Africa was the place the first human DNA was discovered; it contained lots of mysteries, unknown and unsolved works of human creations. He had said what most of them in the Western world often called voodoo were, the mysteries of nature, within the hands of tribes that first had contact with nature and probably God himself.

In other words, the conception of voodoo was wrong. It was how God through the first human race on earth normally applies punishment on evildoers. Voodoo as such could not be that bad if applied appropriately.

He concluded.

John had missed the opportunity to visit Africa as a student, with the exchanged program, his parent could not afford the trip and he had to listen to second class or water down stories of Africa from his colleagues who made the trip, most of them talked about animals, and the people, but he was interested in local beads, the gods, the rituals, and why Africans were not adhering to their faith or religion like others.

John noticed the guy who stood next to him on his right side must have migrated from Africa. He opened a conversation with him, and he complimented him on his beautiful beads and wanted to know more about the reason for having it on his right hand, instead of the left hand somehow, during their discussion the guy introduced himself as the Oracle.

John was surprised how the Oracle explained with details to him all the questions he had often wanted to know about Africa, from his High School days. By the time the train arrived ten minutes later, they had exchanged phone numbers, he told him, he was relocating to Memphis in Tennessee, if he ever had any spiritual or social problem, and he should contact him.

"Just call me." He said.

"I will." He assured him.

That was twenty years ago, they have been friends since, their bond of friendship was solid, he found him very trusting and sincere, his advice on life and nature never failed, he confided in him like a patient would do to his Doctor. He learned more and more about Africa and the people, with so much, yet unknown to the rest of the world.

After five years of their friendship, the Oracle took him to Africa, he was spiritually connected, they visited his people among the Yoruba and Wolof in West Africa, he observed how they worshiped their gods, with palm oil, local kola nuts, the rituals, in the mud plates, the cast of bangles, on the priest, the use of dead animals and bones of lizards to appease the gods. At first, John was scared, but the Oracle assured him never to be afraid,

"Only a spineless man would be afraid of gods in Africa, why should any child be afraid of his parent?" He said.

That was how the Oracle described the relationship between the gods in Africa and the worshipers.

Together they visited the local gods in most of the countries in Africa, the Oracle told him of the relationship between Shango and Amadiora, Ogun the god of Iron, the Oracle of caves which could only communicate with the followers at midnight when everything was quiet, with only the whisperings of the insects, and the Oracle of the of Hills as the custodian of the values of the people.

John was a diligent student; the more he heard the more he wanted to know, he asked questions like a two-year-old kid on issues about Africa. Sometimes, he was surprised about the patience of the Oracle, one of the things he loved about him.

John could still recollect when he asked him why he called himself the Oracle, he laughed and never gave him any direct answer to his question. It was one of his ways of waiving off questions that were not necessary, that, John had accepted as part of the life of his African friend.

The Oracle has since become a very powerful voice on Africa rituals and gods with Cultural Center in the City of Memphis, he had his followers and he was a visiting professor on the rituals and gods in Africa to most of the Southern state's Universities with the Department of African Studies and Anthropologies. He was a man full of energies, sometimes; he would not be around for months because of his job and spiritual stock-taking to Africa to appease his gods.

John was surprised, when he found the note on his door, a note from the Oracle was not a typical message; it was a note that could save his life. He parked his car on the street as he walked to the House of the Oracle, John knew from years of association with the Oracle that he never allowed any of his visitors to use his car garage, they all have to use the street, and he never made any exception, not even for him.

John knocked three times on the door, the Oracle opened the door; John noticed his friend had aged a lot since he came back from Africa, for the first time in twenty years he observed the Oracle had a denture, and he had his traditional white on him like priests coming out of the shrine. He offered him a chair and a glass of water; he added guinea pepper to it, with the traditional local kola nut, and palm wine.

"It was the custom in Africa on how to welcome visitors into the Shrine," He said.

John took a bite of the kola nut, and the pepper, he chewed them together, it was hot and spicy he washed it down with palm wine drink, and it was still spicy in his mouth. He sat down almost four meters away from his host, and before he could say anything, the Oracle beckoned him to follow him to the inner chamber, that invitation would the third time in the twenty years of their friendship.

John recollected how the Oracle informed him Tina would have a son but the gods of Oluweri did not approve of it from Tina to John, the couple had taken the supplement which the Oracle gave them. But what Tina never told her husband was that she gave the same supplement to the Pastor of the Church and both made love to her almost the same period and when she was pregnant she could not determine who the father of her baby was, between PJ and John.

John followed the Oracle inside the shrine, he walked slowly, with some calculated steps, he was aging he could see it from his gait movement he told him, he communicated with his gods in a language known to him alone, whatever he said, it sounded like the rocking of pebbles on the ceramic floor, and when he was done, he explained what the gods to him about his visitor.

"You will need to make the best use of the ugly situation." He said.

"How will that be?" He asked

"Before you could do anything by the customs and traditions of the Yoruba; you must be bold to ask the Pastor PJ questions before the gods would take actions on your behalf and the question must be asked on Sunday during service," He said.

The Oracle invoked the spirit of Tina. He asked her spirit the questions on her son, the true paternity of the boy, her investments and hidden accounts, and others that kept the mouth of John opened.

John was concerned about the response, the spirit gave on his son, and it asked him to contact the Pastors for details, the secret accounts in trust for her son, and the removal of the ring in the left foot of the first lady before he could have access to the millions of dollars stacked away from her years of inequities and loyalties to the Church aside business.

John was confused on what to do next, either to rejoice for the potentials of getting millions the spirit talked of the reality his only son Samuel may not be his, he could not even accept the certainty to check the DNA of his son, because the Oracle warned him not to until he had asked the Pastor those questions the gods mentioned.

That he planned to do.

John got home very late, he was too tired, his life had changed in the last few days, from grieving over the death of Tina to defeat, now to fear and uncertainty that his only son may probably not even be his, just he was thinking

of everything he brought out the house key from his side pocket, this time there was no note on his door, he opened his apartment.

It was all disorganized, every single place had been searched, and his closets, all his coats, and suitcases had been ripped off. The fireproof box which contained all his letters and the vital document was gone too, whatever the intruder was looking for was probably not found, and must have left out of frustration

He called the Police and his attorney, Patrick Zamuba in downtown Memphis. He also thought of informing the Oracle but later changed his mind.

CHAPTER

8

𝔉rom a twinkle in the eyes, that no one else would notice to the slightest curve of a mischievous smile that isn't ready to show itself yet, Wagman was a man who believed your world should never confine you to a geographical location, neither should your investment.

After twenty-five years working for the FBI, that had taken Charles Wagman, to sixteen states and eight countries, he could smell problem miles away or know of it out of instinct, how a little problem could be the source of a bigger one to come. He was going through the routine file on the reports from Memphis in his office in Washington DC when he read about the death of Tina.

Unknown to the Retired Mayor Peterson, Charles Wagman his High School mate had kept a folder on him and as the events of his from time to time unfolded, he updated his records on all his friends, that was his style of keeping tab with all his associates, he had a folder on every one of them. Friends and enemies, he had no exception.

Charles Wagman knew the first night Peterson slept with Tina in Eldorado Hotel; the room was bugged, he was eager to see his manhood again from the video, still the same old Peterson, who derived pleasure from the cries and moaning of his victims.

The residue of the supplement both of them used during the two hours marathon they spent together in the hotel was sent to the Laboratory for examination, he wanted to check if it had cocaine or sexual enhanced medication, but nothing beyond ordinary was found, so far, his friend had kept a clean record, women were just his problems that he knew, and occasionally he was tempted to call him to handle that areas of his life properly.

Why stopped the fun? He asked himself.

Charles Wagman understood why women were after Andrew Peterson, like bees to honey. They both lived in the same hostel in those days and he knew how big and long his manhood was, they had a nickname for him in those days.

They called him *"the third leg man"* none of them wanted him to have a go at their girlfriends, if he had sex with any lady before anyone, she was never going to like you after, and if he did after, it will even make the matter worst as a result, it became the silent war or envy in the school in those days. It made him more enemies.

Andrew Peterson was never in the good book of all the guys, they were afraid of him, but he Wagman was neutral, he had nothing personal against Peterson because his girlfriend was not within the vicinity of the school, but far away in his home town Little Rock, in the state of Arkansas.

Charles Wagman updated his folder on Peterson regularly, as soon as he was appointed the Chairman Board of Trustees of the Pinnacle International Gospel Service; he kept the folder closer to his chest. He knew all the ladies he slept with from the first lady of the Church to the monthly gigs from Tina, he was concerned, Peterson was probably doing it for something far more than sex, there must be more to it than the eyes could say, he quickly assigned a member of the Bureau to handle the case directly, with a weekly report to his office.

John could sense something big was about to happen. But when?

The FBI guy became a member of the Church, he attended the service like a regular guy, he paid his tithes, he was into many committees of the Church and they found him trustworthy except no one knew any members of his family, they classified him as lonely.

The FBI agent name was Payne Wilson, he was a medium built man from the state of Virginia, about forty-seven years old, with a careless mustache and always pulling up his pant from the back and they all wondered if he had any belt at all. Wilson could be lost in the crowd, he had no threatening personality, and they knew him as a man who could clap and dance in the Church more than anyone.

Wilson helped the Church to draft the weekly programs, occasionally, he acted as the secretary for the Church each time the substantive secretary was away, in most cases, the events that made the substantive secretary be away were all doctored by the FBI when the need for a document was urgently needed, the Secretary would receive a call from his son's school and Mr. Payne Wilson would have to cover up the procedure.

Wilson made copies of the minutes of all the meetings, he recorded events and discussions that were likely to lead to a big case as Charles Wagman sensed months ago.

All the efforts by the FBI to nail Andrew Peterson in the past when he was the elected Mayor for the City was futile, he covered his asses more than any of his predecessors, no one knew his secret accounts overseas, he kept more to himself, they called him the *lonely Mayor* since his wife died in a motor accident in Texas. He talked less for a politician, and by the time he completed his three terms as Mayor, his performance rate was above sixty percent, and no one wanted him pulled down.

FBI's folder on him was suspended until he became the Chairman Board of Trustee for the Church.

Wagman also received a notification on the going crime weekly report in Memphis, it says, John the ex-husband of the late Tina of Pinnacle International Gospel Service reported a burglary and missing document to the City of Memphis police. It was recorded and transmitted to the system, FBI got a report and as usual, Wagman got his copy, he moved the folder on his friend from inactive to active, he spread the words around with a powerful memo for the FBI to take the issue of the Pinnacle International Gospel service much serious.

Wagman increased the FBI staff on the ground on Pinnacle Pentecostal from one to two; they were officially directed to dig more into the activities of the Church, the trustees, and all the women sleeping with any member of the powerful house of the Church.

All the paper shred companies attached to the Church gave the document back to the FBI, and they read every line of communication of the Church with banks and donors.

Wagman knew something special that will likely take the front page of new media was going to happen, besides the weekly report was never going to be enough, he thought off.

Wagman wanted to report every 48 hrs. He smiled and said, to himself, time and time again, that very soon it would be time to visit Memphis again; he knew the instinct like it was with him in the Gulf war, Memphis was going to be big news.

He could feel it.

CHAPTER
9

11.07 AM.

In the Pinnacle Church, on the pulpit, Pastor PJ could not believe what he read from the note given to him by one of the Ushers. It was scribbled in funny handwriting, and it was more like what a second-grade kid could probably write, it had not syntaxes of grammatical sequence.

PJ excused himself from the pulpit to the discomfort of the congregation, as he walked away from the pulpit in the middle of the Sermon they followed him with their eyes, as he approached the exit door, they wondered what could be wrong or so important for the Pastor to abandon the sermon halfway.

"Maybe the Pastor PJ needed to take his medication urgently or what could be wrong?" A Lady in her sixties said.

"Was he on High Blood pressure medication? The other one asked.

"Maybe his sugar level went down," Another Lady said.

"I did not know Pastor PJ was Diabetic?"

"Are you his Doctor now?" Another Lady said.

"Maybe he had diarrhea from the way he walked"

"And the toilet is no longer in the Sanctuary?"

However, no one could place a finger on why he left the Sermon halfway; however, to save the day the Assistant Pastor Benjamin took over the rest of the sermon.

As PJ was walking towards the exit door, he was thinking if the message was from his brother, was he in trouble? He forgot to have his International Passport on him that morning and how would he get to the border town of Juarez through El Paso in Texas which was the specific instruction from his brother if ever the law particularly the FBI should be after his tail.

PJ was no longer afraid of the members' Board of trustees after the last visit to Mayor Peterson's place; they were a bunch of girly old men and how all the members of the trustees were scared to death on the document he had doctored himself. What he showed the Board was not really what they signed and unknown to him too, the missing six documents were ripped off by his wife, the copy was with Tina before she died.

As PJ approached the door, he took a deep breath, and he remembered what his Doctor told him about breathing treatment. Smell the roses to breathe in properly and blow the candles to breathe out.

Who cares about the roses now? He needed all the air in the world, he was just anxious about what could be so important that he had to abandon his flock for an unknown messenger outside.

Suppose he had damned the consequences of the note and allowed the writer to come to the pulpit as threatened and that would have allowed whoever it was to display his dirty linens to the Church.

What could have happened? I think I did the right thing he assured himself.

PJ's mind went to the last line in the note in his left hand it was more of a threat than an innocent invitation.

"See me outside now or I will come in to finish the sermon for you" the writer had threatened.

PJ looked at the exit gate outside the Church and the Usher pointed to a man in a car outside the Church almost close to the Exit gate. He walked towards the car. It was a blue Honda Civics, his gaits were unsteady, and he moved like a man who lost all the ligament of his knees, his left knee buckled and he wondered, if it was out of fear or a sign of arthritis, however, the man in the car looked familiar.

He knew him.

The man on the driver's seat was John, the ex-husband of the late Tina, and he wondered why he called on him from his car, instead of being in the Church, even though, he knew John before he got a divorce from Tina seven years after their marriage. He never returned to the Lord and or Pinnacle International service. PJ knew the divorce affected his confidence in the Lord and the body of Christ, the Church itself.

PJ turned on his magic, his smiles, and enthusiasm that had helped in times of difficulties in the past. PJ gave John a big smile that revealed his last premolars.

"Hi. Brother, Lord have mercy on us, I am pleased to see you, Brother! Why are you not in the Church?" He said.

So many questions in two minutes John wondered.

"Cut the crap off PJ, I have just three questions to ask you," John said, with a very icy voice.

PJ did not like the tone of John's voice. Did he just hear him use the cut the crap out stuff, his countenance changed.

"Brother John what happened, the Lord will take care of you, the whole Church could feel your pain," he said in a patronizing way, probably to fake sympathy on the loss of Tina or what else could it be?

The next question from John disorganized him.

"PJ will you tell me the truth if I ask you?" He said. His voice was strained and cold.

"You know as a Pastor; I am not allowed to lie," PJ replied.

"I thought as much too PJ," John replied.

PJ noticed John did not address him as Pastor PJ as it was the custom in the Church. He was not enjoying the direction of the conversation either. He suddenly felt a rush of heat from the side of his head; it was not a blow but the gravity of the next question.

"Ok, I am relieved then since you are ready to tell me the truth," John said.

"Cross my heart." He said.

PJ smiled through his clenched teeth. It was more like a grimace than normal, the question was unusual, more like a man being interrogated as a witness in a murder case in the court of Law, and he could not believe what he heard next.

"How many times did you fuck my wife?" John asked with his eyes as cold as ice.

"What?" PJ echoed.

"You heard me, or you want me to go inside your Church to ask you all over." He said.

"Ummm." PJ hummed.

"How many times did you sleep with Tina?" He asked again.

PJ was deflated for two reasons; he did not know anyone apart from his wife who knew the relationship between him and Tina. If John wanted to know how many times, It was more, John was asking how many times, which one of the several times, was it the sex on his couch in his office, in the bathroom, the three-some Tina had with his wife.

Tina was like a virus, which spread all over his brain like cancer, more like a two-finger victory sign, he had to tell the truth, not the whole truth anyway, he raised his fingers.

"Two times." He said.

"Did you say two times?" John asked.

"Two times," he said in a husky voice that did not sound like his own, it was shaky and husky.

"Is that your final answer?" John again asked with a colder ice voice. It sounded more like a television program.

"Yes! Twice. "PJ said in a husky voice.

"Ummm," John said as if thinking aloud.

PJ kept quiet. He knew how porous and how dangerous his life could be right there in the open, it will be stupid for John to shoot him in front of his Church within the eye reach of several thousand witnesses but he could not bring himself to acknowledge more than two, occasions, the rest could be ugly to mention.

"Ok let us leave that question aside," John said.

PJ's mouth was dry, he needed water urgently, and he sucked his tongue as if all his life depended on the juice or saliva he could squeeze out of his tongue, the next question threw him off balance.

"How many times did you make my wife have an abortion for you?" John asked.

But why is he still calling her his wife? I thought they were divorced years ago, PJ wondered.

PJ felt like running away now, like a thief, there was nothing for him to hide anymore, he did not expect the next question either, it took him unaware.

"Do I need to stand on your *freaking* Pulpit in your Church to ask you these questions before your congregation because I am within few seconds of doing just that?" John said.

"You don't have to go to that extent brother," PJ said.

"Don't you ever call me your Brother again, you this fucking asshole," John said.

"Okay," PJ said.

"What happened to me, I am a man of God, I am not allowed to be untruthful stuff you promised earlier Pastor?" John said.

"Ummm," PJ said.

"Do I need to repeat the question?" He asked.

"Three times," PJ said quickly.

PJ closed his eyes, he broke down, and he wept, as much as he tried to brave up the tears kept coming.

As if the messy questions were not enough, John asked him the next damaging question.

"You slept with her two times and she got pregnant three times, it sounds like a miracle your Church members should know about." He said.

"Have mercy on my soul," PJ said soberly.

"You have no Soul PJ?" He said.

"You have to forgive me," PJ said.

"If the paternity test of my son proved positive that you were his father, I will come for you." John drove away.

PJ was still standing; he could feel all the eyes of his congregation behind him. He looked down, his pant was wet, and he had urine all over his pant.

What did he do next?

CHAPTER 10

11.47 AM.

As soon as John drove out of the vicinity of the Church which left Pastor PJ standing in front of the Church, he went straight home to see his son, Samuel. He found him still sleeping in his room. He had the teddy bear he gave him last year by his side, and the television in his room was still on. John switched it off; he was worried about what the Oracle had told him.

"Before you do the DNA test on the paternity of your son, ask three questions from PJ" The Oracle had warned him.

That he did.

He examined all the statements from PJ, and he was surprised PJ did not even deny he slept with Tina. He had said two times, yet he claimed she had abortions for him three times. It meant they had an amorous relationship more than the two times, PJ reasoned. He hated the sight of the man who slept with Tina with passion.

What a liar!

John could vividly recollect most of the nights Tina starved him of sex. She complained of headaches and problems with her monthly period and like a fool, he believed her. *O ma se o (what a pity)!*

John was now scared of the last hurdle, which was the DNA test on his son, the result of it, could change his life and that of the innocent boy he loved so much forever. He looked at Samuel's eyes they looked very bright, real, and innocent like that of his grandfather, the nose, was like his own and the mouth was small like his mother, for the first time he noticed the birthmark on his left hand it favored the one on the left hand of PJ.

He felt cold inside.

"I hope it is not what I am thinking." He soliloquized.

With a shaky hand John took the phone book, he searched for the DNA test centers in Memphis, and he found six laboratory test centers within 10 miles radius. He went through the list, somehow, out of instinct, he selected Southland Drug Testing, Inc. he picked up the phone and dialed the eight hundred numbers, and the phone was ringing until a voice came up.

The receptionist was friendly; John asked for the best option on how the DNA sample could be collected between Blood and Mouth swap and which one of the two would give a perfectly accurate result between a blood sample and mouth swap.

He listened as she read the procedure to him.

"A DNA swab test can provide enough samples of DNA to test for a match whether it was for paternity or to prove innocence in a crime. DNA could also be tested with blood or hair samples." She said.

"Umm," He said into the mouthpiece of his phone.

"The swab looked like a Q-tip, but it was longer than a regular Q-tip and contains chemicals that preserve the sample. The swabs have a greater advantage over needles they could be painless and easier to use especially when a child was to be tested. Our lab technicians could simply rotate the swab inside the donor's mouth"

She said further.

"I see," John said.

"When the epithelial cells had been collected on the swab, the cells which contain the same DNA that is found in the blood," She said.

"Is it painful?" He asked

"It is not a painful process it is not what anyone should shy away from," She said.

"Okay! Which one would you recommend" John asked?

She recommended oral mouth swab than blood sample because of cost and easier transportation, she was very diligent with the explanations particularly when she said a swab sample does not involve breaking the skin and therefore risks are minimal, but Blood collection poses more risks and could be more invasive as the broken skin.

John did not like the sight of blood.

"Will you like me to schedule an appointment this week?" She asked patronizingly.

"Are there any openings for Thursday this week? John asked.

"Yes: Will 10.30 am be okay with you sir?" She asked.

"I will take 10.30 am on Thursday," He said.

"Please come with two forms of identification. She said.

"Okay," John said and he gently dropped the telephone.

John rested his head on the couch as he perused over the whole DNA stuff, few minutes later, he slept off. He was snoring. He dreamt Samuel asked him why he wanted to undertake a DNA test on him since all it matters was his love for him as his son.

"Does it really matter Dad?" He asked.

"Yes. It does Son." He said.

"And you have to do it?" He asked.

"I have to my son, for me to love you more." He said.

CHAPTER 11

FRIDAY. 10 AM.

The Oracle was in his shrine, in his Apartment in downtown Memphis Tenseness the Apartment was by the river view front; it was overlooking the Mississippi River from Monroe Avenue. He could see the Marriot Hotel across on the Union Avenue street, and the beautiful street of Beale street and crossing 4th Street, and 2nd Street, it was a peaceful and quiet area of the City.

The Oracle could recollect his life in Africa, within the tribe of the Yoruba in Nigeria, which was really close to the small and narrow country former Dahomey now called Republic of Benin borders to mirror the meandering Ogun River. His Great grandfather was a traditional spiritualist, originally from the Mandinke tribe who relocated to the Egba Kingdom in the present day Nigeria after the end of the slave trade in 1833; his mother belonged to the powerful Wolof tribes both worshipped the gods of their ancestors, in future the only child they left behind would join them with his wife.

The Balubas were married for ten years, without any fruit of the womb, until they were told of the Osun River goddess in Nigeria; they traveled by sea until they got to Lagos and they made the rest of the journey by road through the thick forest, they performed all the rituals given to them before they could be allowed to speak to the priest of the Osun Oshogbo, the giver of life to the unborn babies.

Balubas were cautioned about the possibilities of any child given by the Osun, the son that would come out of the blessing through Osun River would be great, they were assured, when the Child turned 25 years, he must return at least every five years to the shrine of Osun to participate in some rituals for higher responsibilities to spread the works of the Osun far and beyond.

That was the covenant between the Balubas, the Oracle's parents, and the African deity of Osun River.

"The child must never tell lies, nor drink alcohol, he would speak for the divinity of Osun River and the powers of Olodunmare in any part of the world, in truth, and in full-strength, even amid temptations of all the western world, his house or apartment must be painted in white and his shrine must be in the back of his inner chamber." The Priest had instructed.

The Oracle kept faith with the policies and doctrines of Osun, he visited the Shrine every five years. Sometimes, he took to the Shrine new converts, and with his good works, he was able to spread the works of Osun deity, one of the gods in Africa with special privileges with the Supreme Being in the way the Black race with the first connection of the human DNA of those who knew how to talk to the controller of human destiny.

He never failed.

They called him *"Eleri Ipin"* the decider of fate.

The Oracle consulted his deity in his Shrine at the request of John and the result was for him to return with any of the smallest pieces of jewelry of his late wife for punishment for the adultery between PJ and late Tina Wilson and only the return of the rings in the left toe of PJ's wife could reverse permanently the negative repercussions on the promiscuity of the Pastor, if any.

John waited for the result of the DNA test. The United States Post office delivered the sealed envelope from the DNA test Center in a two-day delivery priority mail. It was so light and almost as if the package was empty, he wondered how his happiness and future could depend around a noticeably light package, but it was the truth.

John's hands were shaking when he ripped the envelope opened from the left side, and line by line he read the contents of it.

The result of the paternity test was devastating it proved John was not the father of Samuel by 99.99%. He was shattered. He remembered the question the innocent boy asked him in his dream.

He could not tell the little boy the truth, he was confused about his next move and he did not know whether to love him or give him up for adoption, he cried his eyes out, and he remembered the law in the State of Texas on DNA test.

If you fail to check the paternity test within four years of birth of any child, the law will not allow you to even discuss the result of the test. It was not the same in the state of Tennessee, you could place the child for adoption, the problem was too much for him to handle, his head was pounding, and he needed Aspirin or any analgesic badly.

John opened his medication box, in the bathroom he took two pills of Advil PM, he needed to sleep also, he threw the two pills in his mouth, with a glass of water, he swallowed the pills in one glop, he felt tempted to take the whole bottle and even end his life, but he recollected Tina left a note on the secret investment in millions of dollars from her promiscuity with the Church, it kept his eyes opened and hope alive.

He slept off.

It was ten o'clock in the morning when he woke up, he brushed his teeth, and he took a long hot shower, he applied his deodorant and he had a light breakfast with his regular black coffee, with macaroni cheese. He opened the jewelry box he took from Tina's closet. He removed the tinniest ring and the chain, he placed them in a small brown envelope, he sealed it and tucked it in his side pocket, he headed for the Oracle's place in Downtown Memphis.

It was only a 20 minutes' drive from his apartment. He found a parking spot on 4th street, as he walked towards the Apartment, he noticed the different couples walking into the Holiday Inn in the neighborhood, some were kissing, and cuddling each other, and he wondered if some of them were there to cheat on their spouses.

Oracle's apartment was located in a renovated twenty-story brown and red bricks building, John entered the building and down the steps and he climbed the elevator, he pressed the button and it indicated ten floors, the door closed and it moved up with the fastest speed he could imagine, the elevator opened for him on the tenth floor, he came out and walked towards the Apartment marked J3.

John pressed the call button; Oracle's voice came on through the speaker on the wall. The buzz went on and the door was opened. The Oracle welcomed him into his Apartment, and both went straight into the inner portion of the shrine, with a massive display of cowries, beads, and a black chamber pot filled with silky water that could pass for a mirror.

It was indeed a spiritual mirror in which the Oracle consulted with the Osun River goddess and Shango the unforgivable god of thunder in his spiritual belief, the issue at hand was to seek justice and that would be for Shango to handle not for Osun.

John handed him the light brown envelop with the jewelry, the Oracle placed it on the tablet of Shango and made some incantations. A movement occurred unexpectedly, within the silky liquid of the balk chamber pot, the Oracle quickly threw in five pads of Kola nuts and libation of red oil in it, smokes came out, he swiftly removed the light brown envelop from the tablet, he asked John to follow him out of the shrine.

"Do you have any idea where PJ lives?" He asked John.

"Yes. I was there fours ago with Tina for the Christmas Carol." John answered

"Good. This time you will not be attending Christmas Carol there, you will have to hang this jewelry on the front gate of the house tonight when no one is around," he said.

"Okay. Will that be all?" John asked.

"No, it will, in fact, be the beginning of the drama; you must attend the Church service on Sunday to see the result of this covenant with Shango." He said with a dried smile.

"Yes." John nodded his head.

John was motivated by the assurance given by the Oracle; he did not go home. He went straight to the front gate of the Mission House of PJ about twenty minutes' drive, there was no one around, he approached the gate, with his left hand he ripped opened the brown envelope, he brought out the jewelry and he dropped the thinnest chain in it, on the gate and he watched it as it dangled across the driveway, there was no way it could be noticed. John thought!

It was a Saturday evening, he drove back home somehow, for the first time in months, he slept well.

What happened in the Church the next day?

134 | P a g e

CHAPTER 12

In international trade, nobody's hand ever truly cleaned, during his 15 years in doing business in Cayman Island, Patrick the blood brother to Pastor PJ has done businesses everywhere, from Mexico among the drug Lords in Juarez, and El Paso Texas to the Columbia drugs dealers, and the crude oil dealers from Nigeria in West Africa, they all wanted something for something, even the clerks in the office in Africa wanted gratification to move his file to the next level, they called it under the table business.

Patrick knew the rope; most people will say what they wanted, and you must do for them before they could help you. All the frauds, he had been involved with, from bribery to theft by employees, and combating it in most of the third world nations were not prohibitively complex or expensive, it was the way of life.

Patrick could not believe all his brother told him on the phone almost to the point of tears in his eyes. PJ was all he had in the world, after the death of their parents in Brooklyn, New York and they moved with Uncle Pappy Kay to North Caroline before he left home for Miami Florida.

He found himself working for the underground drug lords, after years of loyalty, they gave him his own territory in Cayman Island, but his contacts with those in Juarez and all the cities in Chihuahua (state) and Columbia remained the backbone of his own power within the group.

The news was bad for the Mafia leadership, Vito Lazaro who became the underworld figure of global statue and the most influential crime Lord in South America ever known since

Al Capone, died of a most unexpected death: of natural causes in the hospital bedside at the age of 70.

Vito Lazaro was secretly suffering from Lung cancer, he had collapsed in his home on Sunday morning and by the time he was rushed to the hospital it was over, and the Mafia world had to re-adjust the plan of its business without the prying eyes of the FBI.

Patrick had moved up the ladder, but he was not from Italy, he could only assist, and his stake was a little higher on the ladder. However, he must relocate to New York from the Cayman Island that was the order from the Boss in Milano Italy, if he had to grow with the organization.

It was more of a reunion for him and to meet with the big guys and fix the problem of his brother. He never had a wife or a steady girlfriend; all he had were in most cases one-night stand. He knew all about Vito Lazaro before he went to jail, and he had also package several deals for him, while he was in jail for ten years, and by the time the old man came back, he had relocated to Canada, from the time he was in jail and his years in Canada he had transformed the whole crime kingdom into an unparalleled entity in South America.

Vito was a likable person, he talked with a very polite personality, he loved women, he could talk business, politics and whatever you wanted him to discuss, if you have never met him before, you could call him the president of a multinational company.

Patrick knew Vito demise would bring violent, jockeying for power and position adjustment from the mobsters in South America and he was ready to cash in on the opportunities that would come with it.

The call for him to relocate to New York was not unexpected, he knew his time would come, the League needed someone fresh away from the eyes of the Law to manage the various underground deals, away from the eyes of New York Chief of Police Kelly, one of the leftover boys of Mayor Rudi Giuliani who almost destroyed the Mafia enterprise in the Big Apple City with his crack team squared under then Chief of Police, Kerick Bernard.

When Patrick landed at JFK airport in Queens, New York, he felt at home and almost fifteen years out of New York was like he never left at all, the big Apple City had not changed much, innocent tourists still come to see the high rises building in Manhattan with captivating lights and displays, they moved like ants on 42nd street, they still shop and never stopped coming.

If all the businesses played by the rules of the underground world, Patrick had nothing to worry about. He had to fix his brother's problem first, with the Board of Trustees and John, the ex-husband of Tina; he was almost blaming his brother for Tina until he saw her photograph it gave him a hard-on.

"I can't believe such a beauty died of Cancer." He told himself.

"What kind of man would ask how many times his wife was fucked from a Pastor?" He asked PJ.

"I have never seen that before Brother." He answered.

"And you told him the number of times you banged his wife?" He asked.

"I had no choice; I was not even thinking straight," PJ said.

"What happened next?" He asked.

"He said something about the DNA test of his son," PJ said.

"Are you the father of his son?" He asked.

"I don't know I banged lots of women in the Church. If I must claim all their children, I might end up with sixty children." He said shamelessly.

"OMG! Did you just say sixty?" He asked.

"Yes. It could even be more." PJ said shamelessly.

"You are something else, my Brother." He said and they both laughed.

"You reminded of Uncle Sally and his life with women," He said.

"Really?"

"Yes, the only difference is you are still alive but Uncle Sally, in his own case, was shot by one of the women he slept with" He concluded.

Patrick made one or two calls, the ex-Mayor of Memphis, and the issue of John would be taken care of, he assured his brother.

Patrick had stumbled into some damaging secrets of Andrew Peterson when he was Mayor of Memphis, they were not pretty. Mayor Andrew Peterson had propelled two programs that promised all future contract negotiations involving the City employees would have the right to binding arbitration in lieu of the right to strike before he left office.

He gave the City the power to freeze wages, with no independent arbitrator to determine what was fair and justified, majority of the people said it was not negotiation, they called it bullying, and he had looked into the mandatory retirement pension, which other states or cities ever had.

Andrew Paterson made all the Board members of the City, accept the final statement that would commit the City to more studies around increases to contributions and benefits, his action which was at variance with the doctrine of the party that controlled the executive of the state of Tennessee.

However, as the Mayor, he said his City was ready for new rail services scheduled for Downtown, 47 people were killed in between the time he requested to look into the light train deal, he believed a train service will reduce the crime and accident in the City.

It was more like he arm-twisted the legislature to pass the law that bans the Law school with gay, sex accreditations hurdle, his programs faced lots of opposition from the LGBT in the state; he had the supports of the conservatives, which believed, sexual intimacy that violates the sacredness of marriage between a man and a woman must not be supported by the government.

However, the LGBT believed the law was discriminatory; he became an interesting personality to the FBI, because the threat to his life was apparent, and he was the darling of the conservatives because of his stand on gay and lesbian curtailment in the City.

No one was surprised when Mayor Peterson retired and was appointed the Chairman of the Board of Trustees for the Pinnacle International Gospel Service, that was the place he belonged most people concluded, but in reality, he was made to resign by the Mafia, they threatened to expose his Cayman Island secret accounts and his side cuts from the rail line contract, so he quit.

Patrick was the contact man for the underground deal. All he needed to do was to remind the Mayor of his past, he would not breathe on his brother back again.

Not again.

CHAPTER 13

Mayor Peterson received a call from Gina for a meeting, and he thought of the time they had slept together. She was something special to behold with her *come and do eyes* that often made most men have a lower body movement.

He looked forward to meeting her again. He was, however, surprised when she declined to meet him at his mansion which he suggested. She wanted a different location, something private and secluded outside the City in Red Inn on Highway, and he had no reason to suspect her for anything, and all he was thinking was how to get her laid.

As Major Peterson pressed the remote control to open his gate to meet Gina as planned, it did open and immediately he noticed a black Jeep that slowed down as soon as he was about to step on the gas pedal. He knew something was wrong whatever it was, it was too late to find out. The bullet struck him on the forehead

Mayor Peterson was gunned down by an unknown assailant in front of his mansion, with two bullets in the car he was driving. The assailant had the bullet stock in Mayor Peterson's frontal lobe and the middle of his heart before he died immediately.

It was a news flash widely reported nationwide, the question was who killed the Mayor, after he left office, everyone including his political foes wanted to know why a helpless retired Mayor could be killed. Nobody in the City of Memphis liked the news of his death, including his enemies and the Law particularly the FBI, they all wanted answers and possibly justice very fast.

The following morning Pastor PJ in his car opened the gate of his official house, he never noticed the hanging ring and the jewelry hanging on it, he headed to the Church for the service on the departed and assassinated Chairman. It was what changed his life.

What happened?

CHAPTER

14

The Pinnacle Mission Church was packed full, as it was the last Sunday of June. Many thanksgiving from members for the month was already scheduled for the day, and it was the day most members brought in their tithes and offerings to the Church, and to the community of the Lord only one member would not be attending the service, that would be the Peterson, the Chairman of the Board of Trustees, who was gunned down last Friday, his death was a shock and a big blow to all the congregations.

Who could have shot the Chairman in front of his gate was a strange circumstance to all? However, the only consolation of the people was the promise of the Chief of Police for the City of Memphis, Daniel Frederickson, a war hero of Desert Storm of Iraqi in the eighties, who said, he was not going to rest until he was able to bring the killers to justice.

FBI straight from DC had shown interest in the case also, the congregations believed the sermon from Pastor PJ would be a relief to the Church on the loss of the ever-smiling Chairman with a powerful sermon that would uplift the spirit of most of the people who remembered him for various reasons.

To the men, he was the neatly dressed old man, a fine generous man who was always ready to help, with most of their problems, to the women, his death was greeted with mixed feelings, those he had a one night stand with cursed his white ass, they wanted his manhood would get rotten in hellfire and to all the lucky women in the Church who had a steady relationship with him, it was his manhood most of them could remember, probably the reason why they cried profusely.

What a waste!

If only that part of his human anatomy could be preserved and reactivated most of them lamented.

At exactly, 9.30 AM the Church program started with the beautiful songs, of *"How great thou art Oh Lord my Lord"* and it was followed with *"Onward Christian Soldiers"* the dance was controlled because the Church was not in the mood to overdo it like they were used to.

The women were very moderate with the dancing steps, no serious shaking of the ass to entice the eyes of the men in the Church and the tone of their voices revealed everything about the ugly situation everyone could see the Church was not optimally operating at its highest function.

It was indeed a difficult time for the people of the Lord. But it was fine, it must be a test for them to be courageous and trust more in the Lord they hope.

They prayed and cried like the Jews by the Rivers of Babylon, they prayed for the mercy of the living God, on his Church, they wanted more, they knew what they have lost, it was the political protection of the Chairman from the incoming problems threatening the Church in the 21st Century, the spiritual world was weakening, and the children of Jezebel were penetrating the inner part of the spiritual Churches, they cried for the Holy Spirit to take control.

When it was the time for the announcement, it was also brief, and precise, and it was time for Pastor PJ to stand up for the much-awaited sermon that will bring succor to the heavy hearts of the worshipers, he looked tired and weary himself, he was not clean shaved like he used to do, and everyone thought it was the stress of the death of the Chairman, and many interrogations from the Police and FBI.

All of them in the Church could feel his pain like he felt theirs; the Bible says everything evil shall pass-away; the Church will overcome the problem foisted on the members.

They all hoped.

They waited as Pastor PJ opened the Bible; he greeted the Church and expressed his condolences to the family of the Lord and that of the Chairman that came all the way from Houston and Commerce Texas. He said in less than a month after the death of Tina, the Church witnessed another death, and he asked God for protection and the blood of Jesus Christ of Nazareth on the rest of the Church. He added prayers to every word of encouragement and the Flock echoed back at him with a loud:

"Amen."

PJ moved to the left side of the pulpit, his eyes filled with tears and suddenly his eyes met with John the ex-husband of Tina, and immediately things changed, his countenance changed, it was like he became possessed. He removed his tie, the Church thought he was feeling hot, but the air condition was blasting at the highest level of function, he asked for the permission of the Church to remove his Jacket, the Flock smiled.

He did.

Others greeted his request with *Hallelujah*.

However, PJ did, what was unexpected, he opened the flap of his pant and pulled out his uncircumcised manhood, he showed it to the Congregations; he was shouting "*this is it* "as he was dangling and swinging it to the whole congregation.

The whole scenarios was a disaster, as everyone rushed out towards the exit door, some tried to cover the eyes of their children, all the men rushed to the pulpit, they literarily took hold of him and brought him to the back office, he was sweating and shouting "*this is it*".

The Elders of the Church asked him *this is it is what*?

"*I slept with Tina; her son was mine.*" He said.

"You did what?" They asked him.

"*Some hands are on my throat.*" He said.

It was a problem that lasted for just one hour and PJ's eyes cleared, he asked what happened they could not tell him the details because they too like him were all traumatized by the unusual events.

As soon as the PJ behavior started John knew the Oracle was right when he told him it was just the beginning of the drama to start he quietly stepped out of the Church, within fifteen minutes of driving, he got to the Oracle's house, he knocked his door, there was no answer, he pushed the door, it opened, the Apartment was empty, the Oracle was gone, with a note on his table he said he had relocated to Africa.

What happened next?

CHAPTER
15

𝔉BI Agent Charles Wagman knew Judge Jones Brownville before he ran for the office of Judge in the City of Memphis, he knew him as one of the bad guys in his childhood days.

Because the Judge knew Wagman knew what he knew about what he stumbled on him and some of the documents that could nail his future, he made Wagman's job easier, and he signed most of the FBI's search warrant requests without going through the protocols. He knew better not to ask questions, and it was the unsigned secret code between the two, more like see no evil, ask not evil.

It was Judge Jones Brownville who signed the FBI request to wiretap the homes and office phones of all the executives and Board of Trustees of the Pinnacle Church. It was the second day after the Mayor was shot dead in front of his mansion when Wagman paid a visit to his mansion He was surprised about the document he stumbled into.

Wagman could still remember what he was taught at the FBI investigation class, it was true that dead men don't keep secret, what it was when you are dead, you leave everything to the eyes of the world and you will not be around to cover your ass.

The Mayor had all the photographs' and videos of all the women he had slept within the Church in his house, it was too graphic, and did many despicable things with women and in most cases, he enjoyed how his women cried in pain as he stocked everything in them, he was the dirty old man.

Wagman told himself, the Mayor's private life was not even his problem.

Wagman wanted something that could link the Mayor to the fraud in the Church; he opened the opposite room designated as the prayer room. It was filled with Christian's newspapers and old publications, he felt like kneeling to pray himself because the room was decorated with all that could bring you closer to God, it had ancient rosaries; some of them were longer than usual, souvenirs from Rome, and other Holy ground stuff and Churches which the Mayor had visited in the past.

It had lots of spiritual connection.

Wagman looked around and was about to give up when he noticed the photograph of the mother of the Mayor by the window side of the room. He wondered why he had the larger than life photograph of his mother in the prayer room.

Was it for protection or why would he have such a photograph in the prayer room? He wondered; she could not have been a Saint either.

He thought.

Wagman looked at the smiling Old Lady in the photograph with her pair of 20th-century glasses; he could still recollect her when she came to see her son in the school. Andrew had touched one of the girl's breasts and the Principal had invited his mother to come before a decision could be taken on him, by the panel that investigated the allegation, it was unheard of, but it happened that a thirteen-year-old boy did what he did.

Whatever was the outcome of the case was never mentioned again, the little girl left the school and rumor heard it the Old Lady settled the family of the girls with lots of money but the young Andrew was never rusticated, he finished his school with good grades with his group.

A whispering spirit told him to move the photograph, he did, he moved the painting to the right and behind it, he found a safe slightly hidden, his job allowed him to have a master key to any safe, he took a class in opening safe, which he passed with top grade and he opened the safe within few minutes, he was going through the most secret document in the history of Tennessee.

What did he find out?

CHAPTER

16

Welcome to Motherland

It was the green white green national flag of Nigeria; the Oracle saw through the window of the Delta Flight 425 which landed at Muritala Mohamed International Airport Lagos in the late night of summer.

The flight had been uneventful, he had slept almost throughout the 12 hours direct flight from Atlanta Georgia in the United States of America to Lagos in Africa, perhaps he woke up to use the restroom twice and the food the flight Attendants served, he could not remember, but he reminisced the dream he had, and he was home in the front of his gods.

Muritala Mohammed Airport (MMA) had gone through changes he noticed, as he was greeted with the blast of heavy hot breeze from the walkway compared to the departure section of the windy Atlanta City. It was different.

The arrival section of the MMA was friendly, with lots of commercial posters to welcome the visitors, from the protruding image of Zenith Bank Plc., one of the top 500 banks in the world and that of Guaranty Trust Bank Plc. The City of Lagos must hold lots of promises, he thought!

What a change of weather from the cool Airport in America to warm weather in Lagos, the Lagos Muritala Mohamed Airport had been rearranged and organized with modern gadgets and working air conditioners on both sides of the walkway, friendly airport staffers and an expanded baggage collection section, capable of taking luggage's from six flights arrivals, everything was looking promising for the Nation.

He thought!

The Oracle was happy to be home again in Africa far away from the City of Memphis in the State of Tennessee. He knew it was time to leave the United States of America; the event that happened after he had asked John to drop the spiritual ring in front of Pastor PJ residence was not unimaginable. He knew what eventually happened in the Church was not enough to prevent the FBI from tailing him, he knew he had to leave the country probably for good or temporary and most likely, and whatever it was, it was going to be a payday for the Oracle in the land of his ancestors in which he would be the controller of events, unfortunately, he could not tell John anything. He will have to find out himself.

He sighed.

The Oracle picked up his luggage, just one old bag, he had to travel very light, not much for him on this trip, the major part of his spiritual power lies with his hand luggage, he walked out of the Airport, nothing much had changed since he left years ago, people still hung around the Airport, he flagged down a Taxi Cab.

"Oshodi Motor Garage." He told the cab driver.

"With meter or no meter?" The driver asked.

"With the meter," he said.

"Okay." The driver said with a sign of discouragement, with the meter, the passenger paid only the official rate. Fifteen minutes later, the Oracle was in a bus heading towards Mokoloki in Owode Local Government of Ogun State about 40 miles away from Lagos. It was not extremely easy, within two hours and after he had parted with $50 to the bus, the Oracle was home and paying supplements to his gods with rituals in his village.

What a beautiful place far away from the madding crowd of Lagos or the subtle city of Memphis, everything around him was natural with nature, the trees and the blasting of the wind, the scenery of the trees seemed good enough to take his mind away from America, at least for now.

The Oracle unpacked his bag; he looked around the bungalow of his three bedrooms, everything was still as it was, before he left years ago, except it was too dusty now, he made effort to dust the few areas he could, but he realized he needed a cold shower directly from nature itself.

It should take him five minutes to walk to the River, he closed his door gently behind him and he walked to the river and all he could still remember the first swimming from Ogun River when he was just over 15 years old. He had gone to the river with his late brother, despite the warnings from his Old man never to go and swim with his brother in the river without any able adult or swimmer around him, they went anyway, and he did not know how to swim, without swimming skills he jumped into the river like all the other swimmers but it was too late, after two deeps in the river, he was swallowing water like a fish and they had to call for help, when they got home and his father heard what happened he was mad at him, that was several years ago.

Today, the Oracle combed Ogun River directly with his bare hands moving them like a fish, it was cold, with fishes moving around his legs, he poured beads and Kola nuts into the River which gave him spiritual confidence that all will be well, he gently lowered himself into the river, it was cold and friendly, after all, he had just talked to the goddess of the river with his libations.

He thought!

He swam for almost fifteen minutes, he came out of the water gently on almost wet and on the white sands by the riverside, he sat down, and he was almost dressed up when he had a familiar voice behind him. It was from an old woman with no teeth, she stood like a stone rock, she was his late grandmother, and they all used to address her as Iya Olobi because she sold Kola Nuts in her days.

"Do not be afraid *my dear*" She said.

"Mama Olobi, "The Oracle said in surprise.

"*Emi niyen, Oko mi*" She said in her native Yoruba language.

The Oracle was unable to see her eyes neither did he attempt to look at her; he just knew the voice as he listened. Mama Olobi never appeared to him unless he was in danger, he knew something was wrong or why would he leave the United States of America in a hurry.

"When you get back home check the old room of your father under his Pillow you will find seven cowries." She said.

"What do I do with the cowries?" He asked.

"Mix it with a bottle of palm oil and place it at the "T" junction on the North East of the City" She instructed further.

"Okay, Mama." He said.

The Oracle heard a splash of water, he turned around to see what was happening, nothing except a toad, he looked back, but "Iya Olobi" was gone. His eyes opened, it was then he realized he had been sleeping by the River Ogun side what happened could be either a dream or a trance, whatever it was, he had to check the message given by his grandmother. He headed home to his late father's bedroom, within a few minutes of search; he found the seven cowries under the table mat rolled together as a pillow.

Oracle never wasted time in the past with any of the messages from his grandmother. He picked the cowries, oil, and Canyon pepper and headed to the "T" junction, he placed the ritual across the line, he turned back left as he went back home. It was the supplement for the gods, and he had done his part, let the gods do the rest.

He told himself.

What happened next?

CHAPTER

17

𝔚𝔞𝔰𝔥𝔦𝔫𝔤𝔱𝔬𝔫 𝔇ℭ

Charles Wagman knew he was operating at a level below the capacity of his official responsibilities since he was posted to Washington DC. He needed a breakthrough case to give him the much-desired respect he craved among his peers in DC.

They looked down on him since he got to the Head Office, no one gave any respect to any field operator from the Southern states except Texas, if you happened to come from Oklahoma, Tennessee and Arkansas don't even expect any, those were the states not fully respected within the hierarchy of the corporate office of FBI. He loved his life in Memphis; he knew as soon as he retired from the FBI, he would return home to Memphis for good, to him. DC was full of bureaucracy, too many red tapes and each staff spied on each other's back and he hated it.

Charles was alone in his hotel room in Memphis, he went through the folder on the right-side table; it was all about the Pinnacle International Mission. It was indeed a breakthrough into the ugly business on how the Board of Trustees under the Chairmanship of late Andrew Jackson manipulated the system, far away from the eyes of the FBI.

He wondered how they were able to get away with all the financial mess fraudulently done, without any hint from the government, everything, however, pointed to Gina, the wife of the Pastor, she held the key to the location of the fund, she had since disappeared into the thin air after her husband Pastor PJ was admitted into Terrell Mental Hospital in Texas.

He thought of getting a warrant for her arrest, but he needed more facts to convince the Judge. Charles Wagman thought of the circumstance around the events which led to the admission of PJ into Terrell County Mental Hospital, the report said, he was shouting *"this is it"* all the time and occasionally would pull out his manhood for the public on the sight of women, the same scenario he did in the mental hospital.

He wondered what could have led to this abnormal behavior, could it be drug abuse or overstimulation of his manhood due to excessive usage of performance stimulation like Viagra or Cialis? In all his years with the government, he had never witnessed or read why a man would pull out the topmost family secret in the public and be shouting *"This is it"*. It could not be normal, he thought!

Charles remembered Chike, an African, he had arrested for a credit card problem in Tampa City in the State of Florida about a decade ago, somehow, he had cleared Chike of any possible prosecution and Chike was grateful, he told him, if he ever had any unclear case that needed clarification about Africa he should give him a call somehow the recent relocation of Chike's relocation to Memphis made his job easier.

Charles pulled out his pocket diary, he found the telephone number Chike had given him a few years ago, and he dialed the number, at first it was silence and few seconds, Chike's thick African voice came up.

"Hello," Chike said on the other line.

"Hi, Buddy." He said.

"Is that you Charles?" Chike asked

"Who could it be?" Charles said

"It's been a while; I heard you moved to DC among the big guys," Chike said.

"I don't know about big guys," Charles added

"Don't tell me this is just a social call," Chike asked

"It's not Buddy. I need your help over something." Charles asked.

Charles narrated the events and behavior surrounding Pastor PJ manhood exposure and the shout of *"this is it"* he left out the financial fraud of the case. Chike need not know about that. Charles said to himself.

Chike listened. He said softly, "Ummm"

"What was that supposed to mean?" Charles asked

"Have you heard of *Maagun* before?" Chike asked.

"What is *Maagun*?" Charles inquired.

"Can we talk this over dinner tonight by 7 PM at my Club?" Chike said.

"Sure, I will be there," He said.

Charles was determined to learn more of this *Maagun* if that will be the solution behind the misery of the Pinnacle saga.

"Okay I'll see you at seven," He said.

Charles had four more hours to get to the Club, he thought deeply, of the events in the last thirty days, from the death of Tina and other follow up events that may likely swallow the whole twenty-five thousand members of Pinnacle Mission.

Charles stepped into the shower; he turned the warm water on, the temperature was fine, he exposed his head towards the warm water, the sprinkle of the water on him, made him feel good. He had very scanty hair on his head, only three visible strands on his forehead; he worshiped the hairs like a Jewish Rabbi would do with all seriousness in Brooklyn New York just to hold the Yarmulke or Kippah on their heads. Somehow Charles recollected his good old days in Texas with his long hippy hairs that made him the darling of the ladies in his prime.

What happened to his hairs he sometimes quarried himself?

Charles opened his safe, he brought out his gun, and it was .67 caliper a special FBI silencer gun in which the bullet melts as soon as it enters the anatomical part of the victim, not many of those guns were around, only the FBI uses it when a dirty job needs to be done which will make it difficult to trace it back to the user or the establishment.

Charles drove straight to *Mbari club*, which was located on the East Side of the City, and the frontage could pass for just any third-rated Club, but inside was the heart of the most notorious groups in Memphis next to the City of Knoxville Tennessee, but as far as Charles was concerned Chike had retired from crimes, a legitimate businessman and now an informant to the FBI in the City, who had helped to solve many cases, and Charles was glad everything turned out better for the two of them. He needed no introduction at the door; he was just a friend of the Boss. Whatever he did for a living was never known to the staff and security personnel of the *Mbari Club*. It was a secret Chike kept away from his staff.

Charles sat quietly at the bar, no one paid him any attention except the service attendant, to the crowd, he was just a bored old man with three funny strands of hairs on his forehead, who was probably tired of watching CNN and decided to get out of the house.

He ordered a drink, he was watching the beautiful black lady on the stage with the pole dancing, her movement was very erotic, it was as if she was making love to the pole itself, and the audience were glued in their attention to her calculated movement, her eyes were closed, as she grabbed and rolled down the pole, she was almost naked, with just a little cover of her nipple and underwear.

It was sexy.

Charles realized he had not even touched the drink he was served for the past five minutes or so, he too like the audience were all submerged in the erotic dance of the lady on the stage. Somehow, out of instinct, he suddenly looked around just barely enough to turn left side, he found Chike from a reasonable distance who beaconed to him to come over, and he took his drink and headed in that direction.

The two men greeted each other with respect, he followed him, to his little office behind the Bar, and he was surprised Chike had gained a lot of weight, he was no longer clean shaved, and it was as if he was trying to change his look or personality for something else.

Could he be planning something? Charles wondered: he thought of re-opening a crime folder on Chike, but he quickly dismissed the idea, besides, he had no whispering hint yet.

As if reading his mind Chike suddenly looked him in the eyes, and his question surprised Charles as they both sat down.

174 | P a g e

"Have you heard of a tribe called Yoruba in West Africa before?" Chike said quietly. It was more like a whisper as if someone could be eavesdropping on them.

"Yes, I have. "Charles said.

"Okay! Have you heard of a City called Abeokuta in Yoruba land" Chike asked?

Charles recalled the history class on the Yoruba in one of his FBI training classes, he knew about the years of slavery and how most of the Yoruba who were captured as slaves took with them their religion to most of the South American countries, and how Orisha and Shango became popular in Cuba and Brazil, and some of the Spanish speaking countries and some southern states in the United States of America.

Charles could still reminisce vividly the City of Abeokuta as the place most of the slaves returned to after William Wilberforce a member of the House of Common in Great Britain led the group that fought for the emancipation of slaves in 1830.

"What about Abeokuta?" Charles asked.

"I asked because I have to tell you a story first." He said

"A story about the City of Abeokuta is not why I came to see you; I can Google that on Wikipedia," Charles said

"You can Google it if you like, but this one will never be mentioned in any book," Chike said with a funny smile on his curved lips.

"For real?" Charles asked.

"For real." He said and he sat down properly as he crossed his legs and at the same time he was eagerly ready to hear whatever the story of the City of Abeokuta was or how it would affect his case.

Chike cleared his throat, he brought out the pack of Cuba Cigars from the side drawer of his table, he offered one to Charles and he also pulled out from the side cabinet, a bottle of brandy, he served two glasses and offered one to Charles, he did not take his eyes off Charles throughout, if Charles was uncomfortable with it, he did not show any sign of it. He wanted all the information he could get on the case.

Both men lighted the Cigars and he watched Chike drew the smoke straight into his lungs; it was as if he was in another world. Who wouldn't be with Cuba Cigar? He told himself.

Charles began the story of the Egba he said "After the slaves returned to the City of Abeokuta, they met the indigenes under the leadership of a warlord called Sodeke, because of years of sporadic attacks the city had developed lots of voodoo to protect the people and to attacked enemies of the Egba community, particularly from Dahomey and Oyo Empire.

"Who are the Egba?" Charles asked.

"Egba are the people living around Abeokuta. "He explained.

"I see," Charles said.

"Abeokuta City is their political base," Chike said.

"Ummm." Charles hummed.

"Are you following me?" Chike asked.

"I am," Charles answered but wondering where the story was heading to.

"There was a man who was the son of the most ferocious voodoo man of the City, his wife was not loyal to him, and a neighbor hinted him that his best friend was having an affair with his wife. He was worried, and it affected his life, he told his father, the voodoo man, who asked him to come back in seven days.

He did and his father handed him a little sting, which could barely be seen with the naked eyes,

"Place it on the doorstep when your wife wants to walk out of the room" He instructed his son.

His son did as he was told, his wife crossed the string unknowingly, and later she visited her secret lover, the best friend of her husband at the appointed place and they made love

"What happened next?" Charles asked.

"When the intimacy was over, her lover asked for a glass of water to drink. She stood up from the bed, she got him a cup of water, he was completely dehydrated, he wanted more, he wanted not just a glass of water, he needed a gallon of water, and she obliged him, he finished it, and again he asked for a bucket of water. She was alarmed at his unusual request because his eyes turned red, his tongue was flying around his mouth, it only got pushed back with water, at the same time the lover man was sweating, and he kept on drinking water more and more until he died." Dike said.

"Ummm," Charles said. He could not comprehend the story he wondered if Chike made it up.

" And what he was shouting was like what your guy in Memphis was saying *"this is it"* Dike concluded.

Are you saying Pastor PJ was under the spell of voodoo called *Maagun*?" He asked.

"Most likely" Chike said.

"Is it possible to find a solution to his problem in the United States of America? Charles asked.

"I doubt it," Chike said with conviction.

"How did PJ get such an attacked here in the states?" Charles asked.

"I hear things," Chike said

"What did you hear?" Charles asked.

"Have you heard of the Oracle in the City?" Chike said. With a mischievous smile on his face, Chike wondered if the FBI were as smart as he thought.

"I have no record on him," Charles said.

"I heard he brought some of those stuff from Africa to the Country," Chike said.

"It means PJ was a secret lover to someone else's wife?" Charles asked.

"Most likely" Chike said.

"Are you saying the Oracle gave the stuff to the man PJ cheated on his wife?" Wagman asked

"It could be," Chike said.

"Do you have the Oracle's address?" Wagman asked.

"I have it here." He said.

"You know the most interesting part of this epistle?" Chike asked.

"What about it?" Charles said.

"The Oracle lives in a village very close to Abeokuta," Chike said.

"Hmm! That sounds interesting." Charles said.

Charles drove his car to the address of the Oracle he got from Chike, it did not take him time to locate the home of the Oracle in the City, he moved with caution to the door, he knocked, there was no response, Charles knocked harder again than the first time, still there was no response. He did not hear any movement, but he felt something was not right. He pulled out his gun; he took out his FBI master key, he pushed the key into the keyhole, the door opened.

He did not see anyone.

The apartment was simple; he went through the stuff in the house diligently, from the closet, in the bedroom, to the bathroom, he pushed opened the door which led to the Oracle's shrine, it was full of unimaginable objects from dried animals to roots of all-around a carved object that resembled the skull of a Lion.

Whatever it was, the occupier of the apartment was long gone, in a hurry. He called one of his field workers John to finish up the detailed search of the Apartment, what they found was not only scary, it made the case much more complicated.

What happened next?

CHAPTER

18

Patrick knew he had to find John from the information he got from Gina, his sister-in-law. She was in tears after she had spent the night with him. It was not the first time he slept with her. He had introduced her to his brother to keep a tab on him. They were lovers until she told him what she wanted was a long term relationship. He knew he could not give her what she wanted. PJ would make an ideal husband.

He thought!

PJ never questioned Patrick's ideas, if he knew he had slept with her in the past, he never asked or gave any reason for him to suspect if he knew something. It did not take long before both were dating, he encouraged them to travel a lot and he paid for most of the trips, to France, Germany, and South American countries.

Gina had confided in him one evening that PJ had little manhood and he had no experience on how to please a woman, all he wanted to bang and bang, and within few minutes, it would be over and he would be snoring. He told her to hang on with it; whatever PJ lacked, he would fill in the gap, and that included sex.

That was the secret arrangement between them. PJ never suspected anything at least to the best of his knowledge, and it worked out just fine for her, and he could still remember he had told her she was free to do whatever she could do to keep her relationship going and she could see him anytime she wanted something.

That was years ago, he knew Gina was having her groovy outside the set-up arrangement because she was not calling on him like it was in the beginning, he understood and looked the other way.

Patrick had returned from New York after Gina told him what happened, he made two phone calls. PJ was being taken to Terrell Mental Hospital in Texas; he had told Gina to meet him at Hotel Francis on Station Street in Memphis the day he arrived in the City.

In the confession from Gina to Patrick on the happenings in the Church, there were two graphics on the various deals, banks, and foreign accounts in the Cayman Islands. It threw him off balance, he wondered how she was able to map out the various deals without a background in criminology somehow he felt Gina could be a potential candidate for his business in New York, he assumed.

A confession from John and the death of Tina could be the missing link to finding the solution to the cure of his brother from the voodoo attack.

He thought.

CHAPTER 19

Terrell Texas 10.15 IS

Terrell State Hospital is a 316-bed hospital located in the City of Terrell in East Texas, it is the most advanced psychiatric inpatient operated under the direction of the Texas Department of Health Service mental institution in the State of Texas and probably the best in the whole of the United States of America. It is the Hospital that was to treat and rehabilitate the mental situation of Pastor PJ.

Few weeks before the admission of Pastor PJ into the Hospital, Dr. James Braxton, Terrell State Hospital's Superintendent had resigned with a given one month notice under pressure during a Federal investigation into the problems of the troubled Hospital of the North East Texas Facility. The Hospital came under scrutiny after the *American statesman;* a conservative newspaper reported questions on the death of a Joan Simpson in July.

At the bottom of everything was the $4.7 million Federal money, about 9 percent of the Hospital's annual budget despite the extended deadline on the investigation, James services were no longer needed, he had a month to leave his job.

Dr. James Braxton knew he had helped the Mafia to put away many suspected individuals as psychiatric patients, with lots of medications and most of them were admitted because of agitation, depression psychosis, and anxiety, he had used the anti-depressant and anticonvulsants to silent majority of John Doe in patients.

James Baxton's office in Terrell Hospital had received a call from New York that a PJ in Memphis was to be admitted with no medical records or information that could link his relation with his brother, his name would be John Doe for the record.

However, the Federal investigation had found his Hospital negligent in the death of one of the inpatients, and the Hospital was ordered to make extensive changes by the State of Texas and James had to go, he knew this and he quickly tendered his resignation with a month notice or until a replacement is found for his two hundred and fifty thousand dollars a year job.

However, as the scope of investigations became wider, Dr. James Braxton was even thinking his one-month notification was no longer visible; he wanted to be out quickly. The State of Texas already collected volumes of information in areas on abuse, neglect, restraint, medication errors, admissions, and injuries; the State of Texas was going through the Hospital records now more carefully and in detail, tracking problems, developing solutions, and communicate more efficiently.

The diagnosis of PJ was not looking good either when the patient's case note got to James's table. It was the most substantive diagnosed case he has ever seen in the thirty-five years history of the Hospital with lots of complications, it says a lot about what was lacking in the medical history of the patient, with lung disease, acute and chronic respiratory failure, acute osteomyelitis, end-stage renal disease (ESRD) gastrointestinal Hemorrhage and ventricular shunt status, however, voodoo was not recognized as normal medical problems, a situation that made PJ pull down his pant on the sight of women and the shout of *"this is it"* baffled imagination. He was surprised the patient did not have HIV or Harpies; he placed him on semi-contact isolation.

James Baxton heard from the Director of Social Workers department that PJ's brother was the new Boss of Mafia in New York and he was likely to visit his Hospital, the revelation worried him, and he was to prepare for all medical information that could lead to PJ immediate recovery.

James Baxton had direct meetings with all PJ Case Managers, his primary and specialist doctors, the social workers, and his dieticians, he wanted all the information he could need, as soon as the PJ's brother checks on him.

He had gone through all the books on mental cases, medication, and side effects of each of the medications, after five days of reading and researching he had nothing to present to the meeting, which bothered him. He did not want anything to affect the few days he had before his resignation took effect, so far, everything was not looking good and that scared him day after day.

CHAPTER 20

When Patrick walked into the office of Dr. James Baxton he could pass for a Wall Street Executive. His Italian suite was unique, his leather shoes were shinning and he had on him, a specialized Rolex watch which could be valued at almost One hundred thousand US dollars, behind all this fineness was the ruthlessness of a man who held investments worth over 2.5 billion dollars in the East Coast and South America.

Patrick was gentle with his environment, he greeted most people with his eyes and his bodyguard walked closely behind him as if he was ready to take a bullet for his boss, which was true.

Maria had been the Secretary to the office of the Hospital Administrator for the past ten years. She could separate serious and unserious visitors and those she considered worthy of the time of the Administrator could move beyond her desk, the rest she directed them to Assistant Director, on the next floor.

However, with the size and grandeur of Patrick's imposing personality, she knew it would be difficult to turn him down, besides there was something unusual about the guy, most likely, he could be a trouble maker and that she wanted to avoid, the most important thing to her was how to get back home to be with her granddaughters. She decorated her office with their photographs, they were her only joy.

"Those are beautiful photographs you have here, they must be your grandchildren, "Patrick asked as soon as he sat down in the lobby.

"They are my little angels," She said.

"I hope I am not too late for the meeting." He said in a boring voice.

"It will start in a few minutes. "She said.

"Nice weather you all have here in Terrell. "He said

"We are blessed with lots of heat in Texas." She said with a big laugh that exposed all her beautiful teeth.

Patrick listened with utmost attention, as the meeting went through the medical history of his brother, he knew until he sees his brother, it would be difficult for him to take any decision, most of the time, he was thinking of PJ and the promise he made to their parent in Brooklyn New York to protect his baby brother from any attack seen and unseen, but the Voodoo attack was a different game to him.

"Mr. Patrick, the Director of Social; workers will take you to meet with your brother and if there is anything else, I could do to help please feel free to call on me," James Baxton said.

"Thank you. James" Patrick said.

And secretly, James Baxton was happy when the meeting was over, it was not as tough and as difficult as he had thought, and very soon he would out of this cat and mouse job.

He thought.

The Social worker and Director of Nursing took Patrick to see PJ on the eight floors, the wall that separated the patient from the public was not as thick as it should be but it was soundproof, enough to prevent any eavesdropping.

PJ was not in total isolation, it was semi confinement, and he could still attend to visitors only if the visitors were men, no opposite sex but he was in total contact Isolation when it came to women. Because of his diagnosis, he could not be trusted.

As PJ walked into the visitor's room, like a kid he jumped at the sight of his brother, both could not hold the tears, he sobbed, and Patrick was patting him on the back like a kid.

CHAPTER

21

Washington DC

After months of agonizing on how to deal with the effect of government spending cuts most of the senior officials of the FBI in Washington DC have decided on how they will reduce the bureau's spending: they will shut down offices across the country for roughly 10 weekends of the year since it was costing the Bureau average of 16 million dollars per day to run the locations worldwide.

In addition to the field report, Charles Wagman was given the assignment to investigate the sequestration and how the budget cut will affect the future.

Wagman always kept his head bald except for the three threads of hair on his forehead, he tends toward plain grey suits all the time and almost blue tie. He spoke cautiously, sometimes, with a delayed process to answer to a question for three to four seconds, those who worked with him said; he never said anything until the tail end of the meetings.

However, Charles Wagman was a calmed volcano, a cerebral person, he had the experience that got him respect among his peers in the South, and he could sit through entire meetings without saying a word, just taking notes. And when he spoke people listened.

Wagman's work buddy was Jean Smith; she was from Durham, North Carolina. They shared the same office in DC after he was posted to the Headquarters from Memphis

Tennessee, and they looked and rubbed minds on complex cases.

Jean was more interested in Basketball than Wagman. Jean had a Law degree from one of the best law schools on the East Coast, she once told Wagman that, she did not think twice before entering a field where women were seldom an exception and when she joined the FBI the bureau was less than ten percent women but things have since changed, almost nineteen percent were women, and her ambition then was to be the first Woman Director of the FBI.

Jean Smith was also a loner and single, she worked so hard to the extent that it affected her social life She was given cases along with Wagman that involved Bank robberies and tracking violent fugitives, she also worked closely with drug task forces of Federal agents and local police in some situation, it could take months to build up cases but she never gave up on her dream to head the Bureau. Something will turn up she always reassures herself.

Jean was worried about the new case Charles Wagman was building up on the assassinated former Mayor of the City of Memphis, he had told her, the late Mayor was his High school mate and they used to call him the man with the third leg in those days. She never bothered to ask him the meaning of his third legs because she was smart enough to figure it out. It must be the acronym for his manhood. Or would any man have a third leg? She asked.

"Men are full of themselves "She often wondered why they believed they control the world with their penis.

Most of her relationship with men ended in the fiesta, she wanted more than they could give her and she sometimes contemplated going out with Wagman, but the working relationship would be affected.

Jean knew Charles Wagman had soft spot for her with his pleasing eyes. She could feel the heat of his breath each time he got closer to her, or whenever he shook her hand, he was always warm and moist, a sign of inner feeling of love to her.

She knew it would be impossible for her to date him, apart from work relationship; she kept her secret of whom she slept with to herself, or why did they say the heart of a woman is as deep as the bottom of the ocean! She kept everything intact.

Suddenly the phone rang. She picked up it was from Wagman.

"I may have to stay a little longer in Memphis, "He said.

"Okay, is it about the Mayor's case or the Church?" She asked. She could hear his breathing. It was heavy on the other line.

"Both." He said.

"Have you been able to connect the dots?" She asked.

"It is more than the dots; it is all pointed to a guy who left the State in hurry for Africa." He said.

Wagman took his time to explain details to her, and both reason that it would be okay to contact the Consular office in Lagos in Nigeria to locate and secure information on the Oracle.

Few minutes after the conversation, she dialed a number from a cell phone; she related all her conversation to the guy on the other line.

"Will you join me for dinner tonight Sweetheart?" The guy on the other line said.

"And where will that be Honey?" She said quietly into her Cell phone.

"Club Cabana at 8 pm tonight Baby." He said.

Patrick was an amazing personality; she could recollect the first time they met. It was in the elevator in one of the buildings on 42nd Street in Manhattan New York. The elevator had stopped on the seventh floor when Patrick walked in briskly, he greeted her with a very deep voice, his voice reminded her of Barry White and his bedroom voice, and he looked into her eyes and he flashed her beautiful smile, her heart jumped.

"What a beautiful day?" He said.

"Maybe." She said.

"Are you working in this Building?" He asked.

"On Business." She said.

"By the way, I am Patrick and how may I address you?" He said with a smile on his face. It further evaporated down her heart.

"I am Jean Smith." She said.

She took his extended hand. It was warm and it sent a shivering current down to her knees, by the time they left the elevator she knew she was going to fuck him. They exchanged numbers and he never called her for three weeks. And that kept her waiting and curious.

The waiting was killing for her, as she waited for his call and just when she was thinking it was never going to happen and after several hesitations to call him herself, the phone rang and he apologized for the lateness, he was out of the country on business.

Jean was breathing amazingly fast, her heart and body wanted him as she listened to his sexy voice. Could it be his voice or the way he spoke to her? He knew the right words or how to say it, she never felt like that with a man in the last five years since she broke up with Wendy Lockland.

Wendy was funny, they met at the singles club Bar in Washington DC, and when he introduced himself as Wendy, she was the first to make fun of his name.

"When are we going to meet a McDonald since we have a Wendy here" She had said.

Everyone laughed and to her surprised, Wendy became her friend at the meeting; they dated for two years until he went back to Haiti. He was given a political appointment as an adviser to the President of Haiti.

Jean knew his departure to Haiti was going to be the end of her relationship with him because she would rather stick with her job than to abdicate the United States of America for any third world nation.

Jean had taken the time to run a check on Patrick. He was clean, there was no record on him, no arrest and everything about him was clean, no drugs, no child support hangover, not even a traffic offense, and she wondered how he made his money and that arose her attention to know him more. Not that Patrick was clean, his organization cleaned it up, two dropped murder cases, three armed robberies, and other drug-related cases all removed from his record by the Mafia through the Feds.

The relationship started slowly, he gave her lots of gifts, flowers, and unscheduled trips in his private Jet, he ran an export and import business, he had told her and all his products were approved and certified by the Food and Drug Agency and made in China products.

Despite Jean's glamorous interest in Patrick she never discussed the nature of her job with him and he never asked. It was more of a perfect understanding between them. Both kept the secret of their profession away from their relationship. It worked perfectly well until Patrick needed information to help his sic bother PJ.

CHAPTER
22

On PJ's diagnosis at Terrell Mental institution, it was under the name John Doe to hide his identity; he was diagnosed as having altered mental status, he knew half of his records were not clear or truthful; it was the way his admission could be justified.

Life in the mental institution was controlled with medication; all the patients were given drugs almost at the same time, between 8-9 AM, after breakfast.

The most torturous situation was when patients wanted to use the bathroom if there was no Nurse Aid around, the patients would have to do it on them, and the smell could be horrible.

The law called it, abuse, but who would be the patient advocate in a situation, and those who tried to make a report were given increased dosage of sleeping medication. And in some situations, some were shipped out to the acute psychiatric unit of the Hospital, and in most cases, they never made it back, they were placed under a serious situation which made the suicide imminent, and truly most of the suicide ideation was organized to save the management from being answerable to the law for medical malpractices.

And all of them 30 in number were all placed in the day room almost attached to the sealing was the very old Philips Television that has seen years, it had no remote control and it forced all the patients to watch a boring single Television channel.

PJ sat in a very unusual Conner, which exposed his vicinity to the vast sandy land of the desert around the facility. He could see more than half a mile through the dusty window and if he could still get this mental status alright until he sees women which somehow changed his medical situation.

CHAPTER
23

Eleke Crescent Lagos

Behind his small desk in his office at Eleke Crescent, with the United States of America Embassy in Lagos Nigeria, Moses Darley was going through the vast spread out papers on his desk, from the blue FBI folders and CIA office papers the Embassy received from Wegman's office in which he had to negotiate with the Oracle or kidnap him for shipment to DC if possible.

John Darley US Marine as a Sargent after ten years of service at the end of Desert Storm in Iraq, he took up a Trade officer position with the State Department which first posted him to Accra, in Ghana in West Africa, the population of the country was no more than the size of the state of New York.

Ghana provided no excitement to him, in the way he had hoped, he saw the country more like a laid back nation with the crime was almost zero, and to him, there was no motivation or excitement, unlike his recent posting to Lagos in Nigeria, within two years it was as if he was in New York with the crime rates and warnings from the Home office on security.

He loved it.

Darley needed fun like he never had in his life, this assignment could be it. He had also received a signal from the FBI office in DC to locate the Oracle; the package described him as a Liberian in Ogun State.

Darley picked up his contact list, he called Dolapo Coker who worked in the Governor's office Abeokuta, and his secretary said he would call back in two hours.

Darley had met Dolapo at a Seminar in Lagos about two years ago, and they struck up a conversation, before the end of the two-day conference they were like buddies of many years. Dolapo could converse on any topic. He was highly intelligent, and he had done one or two things for him. His baby brother who resides now in San Diego in the State of California United States of America and Dolapo was grateful. He had told him if he needed anything, he could always count on him. It was the keyword to Darley which he intends to explore when the time arose.

The first time Darley visited Abeokuta to see Dolapo was in April, about a year ago during the Egungun festival and the Ako Ogun events, in which those involved, painted themselves in two colors, red and blue, Dolapo explained the rationale behind the colors, to ward off spiritual enemies like it was in the primitive era of the society. He took him to all the historical places in the City, he loved what he saw and as an African American on African soil, he felt connected to the City, the Centenary Hall, the Palace of the paramount King of the City Alake of Egbaland.

Darley also took him to see the first Church in Nigeria, and the site of the first newspapers in Nigeria, the City was full of historical references and he felt like he had not seen enough of the City the slaves returned to in 1830; He planned for a return visit. He wondered if the country ever had a historical register of places.

The telephone wrung! He picked it up; it was the deep voice of Dolapo on the other line.

"Hi, Buddy." He said.

"Cool Man." He said.

"You sound as if you needed something." He said

"I need you to do me a favor, brother," Darley said.

"Lay it out on me." He said.

"I need to get in touch with a guy named Oracle in your State." He asked gracefully.

"How soon?" He asked.

"Like now." He said sarcastically.

"That could be arranged in the next 24 hours, do you mind if I call you back at the same time tomorrow? He said."

"I will," He said before he hung up the telephone.

That was twenty-four hours ago, he looked at his telephone and hoped for the time, it will ring because he was anxious to read from him, he looked at the clock on his table it was 5.30 pm, it was never going to happen, and he packed and cleaned up his desk. He headed for the exit door of the office, he took the elevator, and as he was approaching his car, he realized he had left his ignition key in his drawer table.

Darley cursed, he headed back to his office, he opened the drawer, he took the ignition key and just as he was about to move out he saw the piercing green light on his phone, someone was trying to call him, he grabbed the phone, and the voice on the other line was that of Dolapo the phone light.

"Will you be available to meet the Oracle later this evening by 8 pm?" He said.

"Did you say 8 pm?" He asked.

"Yes! Do you have a problem with it?" He said.

Zents Sowunmi

Darley quickly recalled all the warning signs given to his group in training about traveling at night in Nigeria.

"Will it not be too late?" He asked.

"That is when the Oracle comes out," He said.

"Only at night?" He asked.

"Yes. At night otherwise, you will have to meet him at the shrine of Osun at Oshogbo later in the week which will be 200 miles away from Lagos" He concluded.

"Okay, I will be there. "He said.

"See ya." He replied.

Darley felt unusual, impatiently agitated. He opened his gun compartment, he loaded it and tucked it into his holder, with his .77 caliber on him he felt secure, a few minutes later, he was in his car, he drove quietly into the night, on the way to Abeokuta about 40 miles away to Eleke Crescent of the America Consular office in Lagos.

Within two hours' drive from his Ikoyi residence on Lagos Ibadan Expressway, through Sagamu he was at Ogun State Hotel to meet the Oracle. He was sipping his wine when the cab drew to a stop and the Oracle came of the car in his simple T-shirt, he looked smart in his black paint and leather sleep on shoes. Darley was halfway on his drink when he felt the vibration of his phone against his side pocket. He pulled it out. He pressed the green light and the caller was the Oracle. Dolapo could have given him his number, he thought.

"Hello is this Darley?" He said.

"Yep, Is this the Oracle?

He said in an exceptionally soft voice.

"I am, the Oracle,"

He said in an exceptionally soft voice.

CHAPTER
24

The previous night was the best for Jean, she was indeed a woman of substance and all her resistance to love had gone, after she had taken a shower, she donned her dress, and she added her makeup, a very light red lipstick which made her lips very tempting to men, she looked great.

The night had started slowly, with the flower Patrick sent, they were twenty-four roses in a gold-plated basket, it had a line stem attached to it, which says

"I will live the rest of my life for you"

She signed for the flowers, and she placed them in her living room, conspicuously displayed in the center of the apartment, and happily, she thought to love him finally found itself into the deep ocean of her heart and tears rolled down her cheek.

She knew Patrick would never let her down like John did with his gang; it was the secret of her life she never shared with anyone, not even her mother. She was eighteen years then and naively in love with Johnny, she told him to wait until they got married before they could have sex, and he was very persistent until one day she felt if she did not give it to him, he was going to walk away from her life despite her love for him.

She was afraid of what life would be like without Johnny. He requested her to meet him at his father's place it was where he had the basement to himself and it was going to be a night for the two of them, all alone.

She thought!

Jean did not tell her mother all truth about what happened that night. She had told her; she was going to see one of her female friends who had a tutorial class for a Mathematics problem, and she wanted to participate in it. John was waiting for her as arranged. He kissed her as soon as he met her at the door of his parent country home on the outskirt of the City his parent had gone to Washington DC for the weekend, he told her.

Johnny's approach to lovemaking was rough. He was like a tiger, and it took him a long time to penetrate the membrane of her vagina, blood came out, yet he never stopped as she cried in pain, he finally pushed his huge penis into her and more blood came. It was painful and she cried when it was all over, but it was not enough, his two friends emerged from nowhere and each raped her one after the other, with John sheepishly smiling as if he won the Texas lottery. He taped the whole scene about the rape and her tears.

Jean could not tell her Mom what happened for fear it might lead to a legal issue and she would be the joke of the School. The fear that the recorded tap might be seen by the public haunted her. She kept the ugly memory of it to herself and she never trusted any man again. That was fifteen years ago.

However, and the ugly event was behind her now, a full-grown ass woman ready to take her future in her hand. She knew all along, as soon as Patrick walked into her life she knew her job with the government and the hope of heading the Agency was over, all she wanted was to be with the man who made her wet all the time, with his voice, his touch, kiss, and inside her, she was in love.

Last week was the most difficult period for her in her relationship with Patrick. She waited for him to call; she waited, but there was no call from him. She had resisted the urge to call him, she never felt like that before as she kept on looking at her phone as if all her life depended on the call, and it was indeed the case.

Love could be very agonizing; it could be a mixture of pain and joy. It could even be difficult to define, somehow, and Jean felt something was going to happen and she was never going to see Patrick again it was a kind of feeling, it does happen, she would never know how to handle it. She made a sign of the cross and with a few prayer lines.

Jean finally picked up the phone and she dialed his Hotel Room number. It rang several times before it directed the caller to the Operator. She dropped the phone, immediately the operator's voice came on.

Supposed something had happened to him, she thought! Or fainted and he needed help she imagined.

She picked up the phone again and called his Hotel number the Receptionist answered the call.

"Hotel Francis! How may I direct your call?" Receptionist said.

216 | P a g e

"Can you direct my call to Patrick in Room 271 please?" She said.

"Mr. Patrick checked out about two hours ago." Receptionist said.

"Did he leave any forwarding address?" She asked

"No, Mam." Receptionist said.

Jean thought she heard a giggle on the other line. Did she just giggled or laugh at her! She wondered. Has Patrick dumped her for another girl? She could not imagine life without him.

She was still lost in space of her thinking until she looked at her phone, she had two missed calls and two messages all of them were from Patrick, and her heart jumped for joy, the message was simple.

" Honey, will you be kind to meet me at the Adolphus Hotel Downtown DC?" He wrote.

"Yes! Yes!! I will." She said to the note, as she held it to her chest.

She was there within an hour, and Patrick was waiting at the table when the Hotel Attendant ushered her to his table, he looked at her flirtatiously out of the corner of his eyes as she moved towards the table.

As Jean approached the table Patrick said to himself she was the most beautiful lady in his life, he had known several interesting ladies intimately in his life but nobody like Jean, and he knew he was madly in love with her.

The background music was soft, friendly, and soothing, as she got closer to the table he stood up, he pulled the chair for her to sit. He never kept his eyes off her eyes, and he looked serious. He could smell her perfume; her light breath and bright white teeth kept his heart beating. He gave her a light kiss on her cheek, she took a deep breath herself, with a light touch on his nose down to his mustache and she felt at home with him.

"Baby, I love you." He said.

"I could see it from your eyes, Sweetheart."
She said.

"I feel like I should bury my head on your laps. "
He said.

"And what is stopping from doing that?" She asked.

"We are in the public and we could be found guilty of ODA," He said.

"What is it about ODA?" She asked naively.

"Open Display of too much attention." He said.

"Does it carry a jail term or a fine?" She asked.

"A fine I guess, but that is not even the case, the Press will rip us out and it will make headlines in the Washington Post. "He said.

"Are we here to talk of the Press or feed me?" She asked.

Patrick pressed the red service button on the table and within seconds, the attendant was there to take their orders. She ordered Salmon Fish with Broccolis, and meat roll, and she looked at him. She looked at him.

"Baby I think we should have the same food, just a little to keep you strong enough for me tonight," She said.

"I want to be strong for you tonight like the Stallion horse." He said with a mischievous smile on his lips.

"You better be, or I will walk away from your life," She said with a laugh.

"You won't do that Sweetheart. "He said.

"Why are you so sure of yourself?" She said.

"Because you love me," He said.

"Yes, I do love you but don't push it too much, Honey," She said with a mischievous smile on her pretty face.

He reached for her hand, he traced it the lines of her fingernails one by one. He wondered if and how life would be without her, it would be too tough on him He kissed the back of her hands; it was a mutual message they both sent to one another, the love was mutually exclusive

CHAPTER

25

𝔄ll the information Patrick got on the Oracle through Jean were all enough reasons for him to visit Africa to meet with him. Patrick knew it would be stupid and unwise for him to use the strength of his organization to solve his baby brother's problem. He had to do it outside the forces of the Mafia without his entire bodyguard except for Stern Marco. He concluded.

Jean had been helpful with his baby brother's issue, he realized he loved her from the day they met and he also knew she would make a good life partner, if only he could persuade her, he never told her about the nature or details of his job more than what she could handle. If she knew how dirty the organization, he worked for was, she would drop him like hot potato, and he may have to kill her. And that he hoped may never happen.

Patrick never volunteered any information either, if you can't find out, I can't help you had been his policy from his days in Brooklyn New York, but he knew, he loved Jean; she was just as elegant, as tall, and noticeable, with her probing eyes and sumptuous lips that kept his heart pounding. He loved to see her dance with the poll in the bedroom before and after they made love.

Jean's passion for Jazz music was different from all the ladies he ever slept with, either casual or longtime relationship, she would flow with the beats and percussion and rolled and curved herself round the poll until she rolled down without taking her sexy eyes off him and which made him desire her more and more.

The flight to Africa was scheduled for the last week of May; it was the latest flight his Personal Assistant Adrian could get through British Airways which means there would be one to three hours stopover at Gatwick Airport in London before connecting the flight 2456 to Muritala Mohamed International Airport in Lagos.

Patrick had told Adrian to book an economy flight to avoid unnecessary attention; so, they could look like any other tourists from any part of the world.

Jean was already waiting at JFK International Airport for him when he arrived at the departure of Terminal 8. She had an exceptionally beautiful navy-blue pant on, a pair of black gold-plated pointed shoes, a snake leather bag, and a carry on just enough for three days visit in Africa, at least which was what was planned. She had that same mischievous smile on her pretty face as he moved towards her.

"Hi sweetie," he said as he planted a light kiss on her lips.

"Can't wait to see what Africa looks like Darling." She said.

"Me too." He said.

"I hope I can see the Lions and Elephants." She said.

"Baby, we are going to Lagos, not Johannesburg." He said.

"What is the difference?" She asked.

"It means no Elephants or Tigers in Lagos." He said with a smile.

"I should have known that. "She said.

"You must have seen too much of Tarzan movies on Africa." He joked.

"What do we hope to see if Lions and Tigers are not part of the equation? She asked.

"I guess we will have a great time over there" He assured her.

"What about food?" She asked.

"What about it?" He asked.

"I don't like Bushmeat. "She said.

"What about Bushmeat? He asked.

"It is the primary source of Ebola Virus disease." She answered.

"They must have something else apart from Bushmeat. "He assured her. They slept throughout the flight to Africa.

Lagos was no different from New York, too many people, both remarked when the plane landed at Muritala Mohamed International Airport, and he could relate to that, he grew up in Brooklyn New York and the crowd from the Airport did not appear different either, except the heat and strong body odor which greeted them immediately they landed. They walked towards the immigration department, a few minutes later, they were out and the Shuttle car from the Hotel took them away.

Not until they settled in their hotel suite in the City of Abeokuta did, they believe they were in Africa?

The couple checked in to Gateways Hotels in Abeokuta from the beautiful location on the hill of the city, they could see the Stadium and famous Olumo Rock. And some of the new overhead bridges in the City. The Hotel room attendant placed the brochures and maps of the City remarkably close to the King size bed.

"Baby, are you not forgetting something? Jean asked him as she turned her face to the attendant.

"I see," Patrick said.

He pulled out a couple of dollar bills; he gave them to the Attendant who gave a big smile that revealed his last premolars.

"Thank you and may I formally welcome you to Abeokuta, the capital of Ogun State, the land of Lisabi," He said before he left them wondering Lisabi was.

Shortly after, Jean went straight to the bathroom, she took a shower, and almost half an hour later, she came out, she looked her best for the Rock City, with a light red lipstick on which made her lips very tempting, he almost kissed her.

Patrick went into the bathroom himself, he stayed longer than usual as the cold water came down on his head. He thought of the contact he was supposed to meet and wondered why the guy named himself the Oracle.

The plan was simple; pay the Oracle the half a million-dollar fee for the solution of what could take care of his brother and get rid of him, which was the assignment of his bodyguard. Jean must never know more than the meeting, the killing would be a separate assignment, clean and clear from the ugly eyes of the law of one of the largest Black nations in the world.

Patrick sat quietly at the right corner end of the Lobby; he ordered a drink and chips to go with it and Jean was still refreshing up in the hotel room, she would join him in a couple of minutes, she had told him.

Will the Oracle come? He asked himself. He was very deep in thought when he suddenly noticed Jean was already seated beside him, she gave him a tap more like a gentle push on his shoulder, and he smiled at her.

"What are you thinking Baby? You are so deeply in thought Sweetheart?" She said.

"Just this trip darling and hoping this guy would show up." He said.

"He said he will. Are you not paying him what he asked for?" She said it was more like a question.

"I am. In fact, I have the money with me" He said.

"Don't worry, he would be here, no one turns away from lots of Benjamin bills" She said sarcastically.

"I see." He said.

"Just wondering how you were able to beat the security at the Airports despite all the partings and searchings' at the JFK and MMA." She asked without probing.

Patrick didn't say anything; he just smiled at her, from the corner of his eyes he could see his bodyguard Stem Marco who could pass for just anyone among the crowd and he never told Jean they were not traveling alone. He need not.

He recollected when he first hired Stem Marco; he was just a street guy from the ghetto of Los Angeles and after five years he had proved himself to be competent and reliable, he must have eliminated about sixteen people for him and cleaned up some of the mess he too created, some were buried in the desert and cemented in the two hundred liters plastic drums in the desert of El Paso Texas.

The plan to meet the Oracle was long arranged by Jean long before he left the States, they were to meet for only two hours in the lobby of the Hotel, like himself too, Jean was eager to meet the Oracle, to see what he looked like, and she had conjured lots of images of the strange man in her head. They were not pretty at all.

CHAPTER 26

Met the Oracle

The Oracle did not come into the hotel through the lobby. He came on a Bike, like a regular tourist, it was not until he sat down opposite Patrick and Jean before they realized he was the Oracle. He did not smile, it was as if he was reading his mind, and that made Patrick uncomfortable, he also ignored Jean and was just as rude, as anyone could imagine, he went straight to the business of the day.

"I am told you have a package for me and in return for your brother PJ in Terrell Mental Hospital in the state of Texas." He said without any emotion.

"Yelp," Patrick said.

"I have this cream for you and this black soap," He said as he placed a tiny bottle on the table.

"How do I apply it?" Patrick asked.

"Take your brother away from the Hospital, at the middle of the night exactly midnight in front of the mission house in Memphis, hire a male Nurse to give him a bath like a kid, with the black soap in a bowl, the Nurse would rub his skin from head to down to his kneels alone with this a onetime use cream only". Oracle said.

"And what will happen next?" He asked.

"The Nurse must step him out of the bowl into a clean white towel, he will also place the used towel into the bowl along with the bathwater, and he must at the middle of the night dump everything into the running river, possibly Mississippi, not a stream, a river and he will be fine." He stressed.

"So that is it?" Patrick asked.

"Yes. That is it, but you must send the ring on the left foot of Gina back to me along with the containers for the cream." He said.

"Do you want to count the money?" Patrick asked the Oracle. He pushed the bag toward him.

"I will not try anything funny with the Oracle if I were you." He said with a dried smile on his thick lips.

The threat and humor were all wrapped in his voice. Jean who had been conspicuously quiet felt like something was crawling under her skin and it was not right with the whole plan, more like they may be attacked with Africa voodoo itself. His voice came out like the sneezing of a black mamba snake.

She felt like going back to the States immediately. She held Patrick's hands tightly for support, her hands were cold, and Patrick could sense her fears. He too held her hands, it gave her psychological assurance, but it was not enough to allay the fear.

"You have my number to call when you have finished with the bath therapy of your brother, not before," He said more like a warning.

A few minutes later, the Oracle took the bag without counting or checking the money, half a million dollars in one hundred bills was the plan, and he left the couple at the bar.

"Get me out of here!" Jean almost screamed as soon as the door closed behind the Oracle.

"I will Honey," He said.

"What kind of man was that?" She said.

"I thought voodoo was in Haiti or South America alone, but this confirmed what I read in a book in the High School that Abeokuta must be the birthplace of Voodoo," He said.

"Did you see his eyes, Baby?" She asked.

"The two eyes were different; it was like he had the eyes of a Lion and snake at the same time." He said.

"When is our flight back to the States? She asked.

"I had arranged for us to see Olumo Rock." He said ignoring the flight time she asked for.

"I am not interested in any fucking Olumo Rock. Just get me out of here or Let us move to Lagos tonight, there is no civilization here." She demanded.

"We are leaving in a few minutes sweetheart," he said.

CHAPTER

27

Dan Aboki was a ten years veteran agent for Nigeria Security Services; his age could not have been more than forty years, he was with the Nigeria Army intelligence contingent to Liberia and Sierra Leone wars over blood diamond, when he was discharged from the Army he joined the Nigeria Security Services.

Dan sat quietly watching and listening to the conversation of Patrick and Jean. For the sum of one thousand naira, he had through one of the waitresses planted a bug under the table and bedroom of Patrick and Jean. He had listened to every word of their conversation last night and he was amazed about the erotic mourning of their lovemaking process; he wondered how these Americans learned the dirty words they use in the bedroom, as much as he never wanted to make it his business, he found himself admiring some of their frolics and small bed talks.

Dan assigned duty by Security Service command was to watch and report any foreigner in any of the hotels in the City of Abeokuta since the missing Diplomat case was mentioned at the last meeting.

Any arrest or breakthrough could lead to a promotion for him and sitting there watching the American couple, he could not believe the visit of Jean and Patrick had something to do with the abduction of the Diplomat, if he could crack this case, he wondered how he would look on the television addressing the press, and television stations.

Suppose the news came out on CNN, MSNBC, FOX News, and Aljazeera America? He asked himself.

"I better start writing my speech that would make me look good," He said almost aloud to himself.

Dan could not believe his luck, that this couple that could pass for just innocent tourists holds the key to his fame, but there was something strange about Patrick, his eyes looked deadly and he wondered why he did not make any phone calls since they checked into the Hotel, unlike most foreigners that would make several calls.

Were they running away from something? That he intended to find out. Stay focus. He told himself this could be the replacement for the missed diamond opportunities he thought he could not get for going to that stupid Liberia and Sierra Leone wars.

The worst part of it was his wife, she did not believe he did not get the diamond, her friends, and family were waiting when he came back from the war, when he told them he had no diamond, they called him a loser. He never forgave himself; maybe this case would earn him the respect of his family and friends he assured himself.

Dan found Patrick was talking to a man who could be in his sixties, they had shifted from the bugged table to the bar, which made it difficult for him to eavesdrops on their conversations, he noticed they exchanged bags and both seemed to be smiling as if he was assuring Patrick of something, whatever it was, it must be in the bag Patrick got from the other man.

As soon as the conversation was over and the elderly man walked out towards the door, he followed him with his eyes, he noticed a short man around five feet six talks followed the old man, he looked like a foreigner, he could sense danger, five minutes later, the short guy was back with the same bag the elderly man had a few minutes ago.

Dan sprinted to his feet quickly like a man chasing something; he walked out of the Hotel towards the parking lot to find out if something had happened to the Old man, he was just lucky enough to catch a glimpse of the Old man with his bag on the driver's seat just as he drove away in his car and the Bike neatly attached to the hood of his car

Something was not right. Dan told himself. He walked back to the Hotel. Patrick and Jean were long gone, their table was empty, and he looked around, no sign of the couple. He blamed himself for letting Patrick and Jean out of his sight. He took the elevator to the fifth floor of the hotel; he stepped up his movement like a soldier and turned right towards room 517 which was the room Patrick and Jean had stayed.

Dan knocked on the door, there was no response the door was locked, he knocked again and announced himself as a room attendant, still, there was no response he used his master's key to open the door. It opened, he took out his gun, and he moved quietly inside the room, he had his gun .32 calibers on him now, and he felt secure. He thought of calling for backup but changed his mind. It would probably be too late. He moved up the silencer clipped to the head. He heard a sound on his right side, just as was about to turn right something heavy landed on his head, and he went blank and fainted.

Patrick had seen the movement of Dan Aboki from the time he walked into the hotel lobby, it was the reason he shifted his table to the next one, out of instinct, and by the time Dan followed Stein Marco out of the Lobby his suspicion was confirmed, he knew they were being tailed, he asked jean to follow him out of the Lobby and he was glad she never asked any question.

"Baby we need to get out of here faster than we can." He said.

They moved like the speed of light and within seconds they were in their rooms with everything packed. He moved Jean into the Closet and Patrick pulled out his gun and was ready behind the door until Dan Aboki walked in.

Patrick went through Dan's pocket, he found his SSS identification and a couple of US dollars in twenty denominations, he forced Dan mouth open, and he tucked in all the dollar bills and his identification card in his mouth.

Patrick took a bewildered Jean's right hand and both walked out of the Hotel room towards the reception and a few minutes later they were on the way to the Lagos Airport, the driver, and the car to take them to the Airport was waiting at the Lobby.

Unknown to Jean, the bodyguard, Stern Marco, was the same Cab driver who took them to the Airport. Within 45 minutes Patrick and Jean were at MMA in Lagos and they barely made it through the immigration process when the flight was announced to be on schedule.

Stern Marco, Patrick's bodyguard had hijacked the Cab from one of the drivers in the hotel, he tied him to the male bathroom and injected a sleeping medication drug to the side of his neck,

"He would probably be up and going after six hours." He soliloquized.

Stern Marco had a weakness he never struck any of his victims fainted without leaving a thank you note, also placed five hundred US dollars in his pocket probably for the rental of the Cab with a note which asked the driver to pick his cab up at the Airport with a thank you note.

As soon as Patrick and Jean got down from the cab, at the Airport, they moved to the departure gate Stem could not wait to see what was in the bag he had exchanged at gunpoint from the Oracle. He was surprised, the Old man never resisted him, he gave him the bag willingly with a smile and he had even had a fired a shot at him, but to his surprise, it had no effect on the old man. He told him to go away before something terrible happened to him.

"What gave you the impression that the little toy in your hand can kill the Oracle?" He asked as if easing out like a snake.

"What?" Stein Marco said in confusion.

Stern Marco was disturbed, he had killed lots of people in his life, short, tall, Asians, White, and Blacks but never in his life had his bullet failed to have any effect on any of his victims.

Could it be the technical fault of his gun or voodoo? He knew better not to experiment with the man who could stop his bullet with something probably spiritual or what could it be? He backed away with his dirty hand holding tightly to the bag the Oracle held before.

At Lagos MMA Airport, Stern Marco wanted to know what was in the bag himself before he could join the flight. He took the bag with him to the bathroom, if it contains lots of money; he may have to ditch his boss and relocated to Columbia. He heard the country of Columbia is noted for two things, white and Black powders. Who cares about the coffee Black powders, he wants to be involved with White powder, the cocaine?

"That was where the big money was." He told himself.

As the last user in the restroom walked out, Stein closed the door gently behind him and he unzipped the brown leather bag, without looking inside it, he combed it down deeply with his left hand, he felt something very cold like the tip nose of German shepherd dog, he knew of hot money, not cold dollar bills, something must be wrong he thought.

As he was about to pull out his hand, he felt a sharp bite on his tomb like a pin, and whatever it was in the bag raised its head out of the bag on him, it was a snake, the black mamba, with a splitting ferocious tongue.

Stein Marco never had any direct encounter with snakes in his life, though, he had read all about snakes and now directly looking at the Black mamba, he knew why they call Africa a jungle. He knew he was going to die; he was too dazed to have confidence in his gun after it failed him with the Oracle.

The snake struck Stern Marco four times in rapid successions on the tip of his nose, and his left eye. He cried out loud, but there was no one around to help. A few minutes later, he was foaming and very weak to move his legs. He was dead all alone in the toilet.

Patrick noticed Stein's name was mentioned several times, through the public service system by the airline's official to join the flight. Until they were all boarded on the plane, Stein Marco was a no show and that was the last time he set his eyes on him, three days later he read in the Dallas

Morning News of a male foreigner found dead of a snake bite in Airport restroom in Nigeria Africa, the description fitted Stern Marco.

It was time to shop for a replacement. He said to himself.

CHAPTER
28

𝕬ugust 20ᵗʰ 𝖂ashington 𝕯𝕮

The kidnap case of the United States of American Commercial Attaché, Retired Sergent Darley in Abeokuta, in Ogun State was up in the news all over the United States of America and the western world. Like a wildfire in the savannah, the news spread along with the Ebola virus news it was the number one news in the first world nations.

All the major cable news CNN, Fox News, MSNBC, and Aljazeera America made the kidnapped story number one; they repeated the news every ten minutes as if a new revelation would happen, but nothing happened.

The talk show hosts made a big deal of the kidnapped story also, some went down the memory lanes of what happened in Kenya in 1972 and South Korea in 1978, analysis and comparisons were drawn and it embarrassed the presidency in Washington DC.

It was another opportunity for the conservatives in the South to get at the presidency. They believed he was not competent, they have never accepted the legitimacy of his presidency, his immigration policy, and gun control Laws had been dragged to the Supreme Court and in most of the cases, and he had won with little damages to all the laws that almost considered as if all the amended sections of Constitution would be affected.

The Presidency had just recovered from the Libya Benghazi tragedy and was worried, with the midterm elections looming, he wanted to regain the Senate and House of Representatives for his Party, but the polls were not looking good either.

It was the year for the midterm elections; most of the members of Congress from his Party were very reluctant to have a President Chris Candlewood on their campaign or fund-racing programs. His gay right policy was the major reason why his job approval rating was nose-diving, he should not have done it, the Polls said so. But he did and his party may have to pay for it in the midterm election.

The mess President Chris Candlewood met was horrible when he took over the Administration, with three wars, and the effect of Obama care, which had been weakened by many legal pronouncements from conservative Judges, he had even won the Presidency by just five thousand votes, the least votes in the last one hundred and fifty years of any presidential elections in the United States of America, after two years in office his health had deteriorated like the health care policy of his predecessor, it was a secret known to him and his primary care provider, Dr. Mark Jason alone.

President Chris Candlewood did not fully reveal the details of his health to his wife also. He had made up his mind not to run for re-election after his Party lost the control of the Senate and House of Representatives which made his government vulnerable to the oppositions and conservatives.

What was the purpose? He asked himself, if the Press ever knew the extent of his health problems, he would be toasted. The legacy of his presidency would however depend on how he handled the missing Diplomat in Africa.

President Chris Candlewood had called on the Nigeria President Dr. Boniface, and he promised to get to the root of the matter, but he could not even bring himself to believe any promise from any African leaders, but as soon as the Congress approved the aids for Nigeria like any other nation, he would exact more pressures on the leadership of the country. It was his only hope of dealing with one of the most developing countries in the third world.

Congress was not happy either, with his aids policy to Africa, they wanted him to tie it to accountability and the Republican Party had also demanded that the projects on which the aids were meant should be done by American contractors.

President Chris Candlewood knew that policy would not fly with the rest of his Party and Black Caucus whatever, it was; he was already looking forward to the last days of his presidency with contentment.

However, the CIA and FBI report indicated unofficially, that Agent Darley who was attached to the Consular Office in Lagos had on his own will traveled to the City of Abeokuta to negotiate with the Oracle, who suddenly left Memphis after the unusual altered mental status of one Pastor PJ of Pinnacle Pentecostal mission in the State of Tennessee. The report said.

The report revealed the Oracle was a Green cardholder; Homeland Security had even written to him to be an American Citizen more than four times after 23 years in the country with a good record, with no default in his business and payments, surprisingly, the report stated he declined all the invitation.

The President pushed the black button under his desk; he talked into the microphone to his Personal Assistant.

"Put the President of Nigeria on the line for me," He said.

"Roger. Mr. President." His Secretary said.

CHAPTER
29

𝕿he People of the Federal Republic Nigeria had gone through lots of political and social upheavals in the last twenty-five years due to years of Military rules and dictators which denied the people of their basic rights and many of the citizens had left the country for greener pastures.

The new civilian President, Dr. Boniface from the minority with his resource control hat was faced with challenges of rebuilding the country from the ruins of the military in the eighties and several attacks of Boko Haram from the North East of Nigeria but things were gradually getting better for the new President, several years of debates and marathon debates were over, the President could now settle down to do the work of the people.

The president was a quick learner, and it did not take him a long time to time understand the extraordinarily little he could do as a President despite the massive votes he received from the youths. It was hopeless trying to please everyone, and he may have to pick his priorities.

The President's desk was full of unusual requests, mostly favors from political associates and Unions on strikes and looming strikes from the Petroleum marketers. The previous night meeting with Representatives from China had gone into extremely late in the nights and he was tired; President Boniface had to drink two cups of coffee with creamer and four sachets of sugar to stay awake that morning. He was exhausted. "One term was enough for him" he reasoned with himself.

The Presidents would be the first in the history of the country to go through a divorce process. It happened as soon he was announced as the winner of the Presidential election. His wife warned him to stay away from presidential politics all she wanted was the wife of the Governor not the first lady of the country, Boniface had jettisoned her views and instead of a congratulation note or card from his wife, she filed for a divorce.

However, on the left corner of his desk, he pulled the folder on the American Diplomat that was kidnapped. The folder was tagged and marked urgent by the Inspector General of Police. He opened it up; it stated that the Commercial Attaché of the American Embassy Darley was abducted the previous night in Ogun State. He was last seen with a staff of the State Government at Ogun State Hotel.

However, Zone 2 of the Federal Police in Abeokuta did not give a detailed report, except the matter was urgent and still under investigation. And the nosey Press had asked the Presidency why the IG was keeping his job.

President Boniface knew his trip to the United States next week would have to be shelved to save him from the eyes and ugly questions of the American Press, the kidnapped case must be resolved quickly.

The telephone conversation with the President of America however, revealed more than just the Kidnap case, his presidency in America was also on the line, and he could feel the pain of Chris Candlewood the President of the most powerful nation on earth.

The upcoming trip of President Boniface to the United States of America had also attracted comments from the opposition Social Democratic Investment Party, the pressure on him was to reduce his entourage from 120 to 40 and he was still considering the opposition's request on the size of his crowd when the issue of kidnap case came in. He pushed the button on his table and his Assistant came in quickly.

"Ask the IG to come immediately." He said.

"Roger Mr. President." He said.

"And Chief Security Adviser too." He quickly added.

"Roger Mr. President." He said again.

Twenty minutes later, the two men sat with the President to discuss the kidnapped case of the American Commercial Attaché Darley.

The President cleared his throat, he needed his favorite alcohol drink by now because the caffeine in his coffee, he had in a few hours ago had expired from his system which affected his ability to stay awake without dozing off, and he needed something stronger.

President Boniface excused himself to use the restroom before the meeting could start. It was the place he had hidden the bottles of all his assorted alcohol, Brandy, Vodka, Whiskey, and many assorted drinks. He liked the display look and arrangement of all the drinks in his secret collections. They look fine to him; he smiled at the collection of the drink and wondered what the world would like without drinks.

President Boniface ripped opened one of the bottles, it was the Whisky from Germany and still with a smile on his face, he took a larger size than his usual cup full, he globed it at a time, in his mouth, it burnt down his throat and his eyes were wide opened, he felt he could look anyone in eyes with the effect of the alcohol in his system. He threw two strong mint into the corners of his mouth and rolled them side to side to remove any traits from his breathe the smell of the Vodka drink.

In the office of the President, the two top security advisers were discussing cautiously, the kidnapped case of an American Diplomat.

The IG knew his proposed vacation was already off the table. He cursed and hissed inwardly, without showing it on his face, while the Chief Security Adviser Retired General Apitipiti knew his days were numbered too since the Press felt he was not competent enough to handle Boko Haram insurgents.

Some members of the National Assembly Security Committee chaired by his sworn enemy Dr. Tinuwada were already calling for his resignation, he knew he was not going to last another thirty days in office, if he could not come up with any viable solution to the Islamic resurgences in the North East of Nigeria, to be fair to himself, he had no solution on how to handle it, he just plans to roll with it, and that will not be enough, they needed result.

As soon as President Boniface walked in, both men stood up, they noticed his eyes were red and his gait looked unsteady, they dare not ask question or joke with him, maybe if they were friends before he ran for office but there was nothing like that, their jobs and political future depended on the president and result.

"Sit down Gentlemen." The President asked the men.

They sat down as soon as he sat down himself; he wanted to know how soon the kidnapped case would be resolved. He gave the two men forty hours to resolve it, and he said, he wanted to look good during his trip to see President Chris Candlewood in the United States of America if it could be salvaged, a trip that included his annual medical checkup. He told them further of the telephone conversation he had with the President of the United States of America.

President Boniface was also a good listener, he took notes like a student in the school, and he had that funny smile on his face and appearance of innocence even when he was about to get rid of any of his staff.

Both men contributed to the discussion and it was resolved a special crack team be created to handle special cases outside the establishment but the fear of the crack team turning into a killer squared itself like the era of General Sanni Abacha also came for discussion.

The last Inspector General was very flamboyant, he played on words each time he was in a meeting with the President, but the day he was fired, he was still talking in his Oxford English syntax until the President passed him a short note, he did not read it and he was still talking until he got the second note, he looked at it and it said, "*Please get out of my office*" he could not finish his sentence, he collapsed and he was rushed to the Asokoro Federal Medical Center. It was the place he completed his disengagement papers and when he recovered fully, he retired to his village and he was never seen in the public again.

IG Kosoko was his replacement for the past eighteen months and now he felt he had better resigned quickly instead of allowing the Press to make fun of his big tummy after a sack letter, the stress was all over his face and he did not have good news from his Doctor either, the slim fit Doctor Mac May.

It was easy for anyone to be slim and fit like his Doctor, who had told him to stop eating beef, no sugar, no sodium in any form, no starchy food, he was even told not to drink his regular palm wine, secretly, he felt he was in a perpetual stomach infrastructure jail. He cursed.

Thirty-two years of service was enough, IG Kosoko concluded, he looked the President in the eyes, and he said.

"Mr. President I thank you for the opportunity you have given me to serve the nation, at this time. Your Excellency, it is time for me to be with my grandchildren and my sick wife." He said.

"Do you still need time to think over this or you just got burnt out by the Boko Haram case?" The President asked as if he was teasing him.

"Mr. President I guess I am done; I wouldn't be as effective as you would want me to be if I stayed." He said.

"I will respect your decision, but if there is anything you need from me, my office is always opened to you." He said.

"Thank you. Mr. President." He said.

Both men shook hands while the National Security Adviser Dan Suleiman looked on. IG Kosoko walked out briskly, and Dan Suleiman knew all along the President was about to fire the IG in the next two days if he had not resigned and he had secretly given him a tip on it. It appeared he had beaten the President to the game. He got his information from the female secretary in the presidency; he slept with her regularly to keep a tab at the presidency.

It cost him a couple of thousands per month. The information she gave was good enough for the price and excitement, aside, she never gave him too much demand except for him to ensure the promotion and career of her brother.

IG Kosoko served in the Military with Dan Suleiman in their early careers days, and they have done so many precarious things together, women, drinks, and drugs, and it would be unfair if he had not given his friend a tip on how to quit before the President could disgrace him out at the next Federal Executive meeting scheduled for the following day.

By the time Dan Suleiman looked up he found the President was staring at him directly, he felt uncomfortable.

"Did he suspect he gave the IG a hint on when to quit?" He asked himself.

"That was fast." President Boniface said with a thin smile.

"I thought so too. Mr. President." Suleiman said with a straight face.

"How could he have known he was almost on his way out? "The President asked casually.

The President offered Suleiman a Cuban Cigar, he took it, just as he rested his head on the back of the chair and he was surprised his right hand was steady, but his left eye was twinkling. He noticed the President eyes never left his forehead as he dragged in the smoke of the Cigar into his lungs; at the same time he combed his mouth with his tongue, he recollected what his Doctor said about any respiratory damages to the lungs, if the vital capacity was damage.

Dr. Jason had this unusual way of passing medical information to his patients, he would say it in an amazingly simple way that even kindergarten kids could understand it.

"You only need twenty-four percent out of a full capacity of the air you drag into your lungs that will be converted to useable oxygen the rest would be turned to Nitrogen which no one needed." Dr. Jason said.

"I see." He replied.

The Doctor told him to blow the candle, and smell the roses, it was his ways of asking his patients to breathe in and breathe out.

Retired General Dan Suleiman was still standing with the eyes of the President gazing at him, all the respiratory tricks from Dr. Jason did not apply to the current situation, he was sweating profusely from his armpit, and if he was given the chance he was ready to blow away all the candles in the world, or smell the damn fucking Roses just to get away from the gazing eyes of President Boniface.

"If we can't find the guy who kidnapped the Diplomat in the next forty-eight hours, I may have to reshuffle my cabinet," He said quietly, and he was still Combing his mouth with his tongue.

Suleiman did not say anything. Or what did the President expect him to say? Did he expect him to say okay get rid of everyone and keep him or plead on behalf of others that he should not do it?

The next question from the President took him off guard.

"Where were you last night at around eight o'clock?

"Eight O'clock. Mr. President?" He repeated.

Suleiman was buying time to be able to compose any lie he planned to unleash out.

"Yes. Eight O'clock." The President repeated the time and, of course, he heard the question, he was thinking about what to say.

"I worked late into the night Mr. President; I was right here in the office." He said.

Dan had an uncomfortable thin smile on his lips and his left eye was blinking up and down.

"What happened when you left here last night?" President Boniface asked quietly and deadly.

Dan Suleiman did not like the direction of the interrogation and it was difficult for him to ask the President to tailback, it was more than being on the witness stand and being interrogated by the late aggressive Lagos Lawyer Gani Fawehinmi.

"I crashed by my girlfriend's place on Maitama Sule Way for about two hours." He said.

Everything was looking more like a confession in front of a Catholic Priest or what will he ask next? Will the

President ask him if he slept with his girlfriend or what? He was thinking.

"I did not know you have the same girlfriend with the IG Kosoko because he too was around the same place as you." He said.

"So, the Bastard knew my movement. "He thought. Suleiman kept quiet.

The next question from the President was unexpected; he was not prepared for it either.

"How long have you been working for me?" He asked.

"From the time you were Governor of Edo State." He replied.

"Why did you have to lie to me?" He asked.

"I am not following you. Mr. President." He said.

"Did you tell IG Kosoko he was going to be relieved of his duty post on Wednesday?" He asked.

President Boniface asked with a straight face. Dan Suleiman kept quiet, he felt his lies were becoming too many and he was going to need another couple of lies to cover the previous lies, whatever remains to his integrity, he intended to keep it, probably with his mouth closed. He could not even tell the President he got his information from Amina in the office of the President. She was his fuck Buddy.

President Boniface had an unusual way of getting information from his surrogates or ministers, he hired ladies in his office to sleep with them, they, in turn, thought they could sneak information about him from the girls while in reality, they were double agents for him, it was through this source he had been able to keep his troubled presidency afloat.

"Do you want my resignation letter, Mr. President?" He asked.

"That will be the right thing to do Dan Suleiman." He said with a tight lip.

Immediately the President addressed him by his full name, he knew he was toasted, there would not be any going back he was already history to his administration.

"Thank you, Mr. President, for the honor to serve the nation under your leadership. "He said.

"You are most welcome." The President replied.

Suleiman walked out of the presidential office, he was in a very deep thinking mood, when he passed through the main, entrance he noticed a car pulled in, it was his one-time Deputy's car, the bastard knew all along it going to be his last day in office.

He was not surprised when the government-controlled Nigeria Television Authority NTA televised the appointment of a new National Security Adviser that evening. It was General Josey Igodalo his onetime deputy

CHAPTER

30

$$$ office in Lagos

Major General Josey Igodalo was almost six feet tall, about forty-two years old, he was never married, and he had fathered a child out of wedlock when he was a teenager and the mother of his child had run away with his son due to the irrational behavior of a teenage Josey Igodalo.

Josey as he was fondly called by his peers never met his father, his mother told him his father ran away, the truth was

Josey was born a bastard; his mother was a street lady in her time. She slept with anyone with money and drugs. When she became pregnant, she could not identify who the father of her son was. She later committed suicide when her son turned eighteen, and it was the year Josey joined the military.

Josey Igodalo grew up never to trust anyone; in most cases, he started his relationship with people on the level of midst rust to trust, but in fact, he never really gotten to the trust level.

He walked as if he had springs on each of his toes, his eyes were always alert and red, and he screeches them as if he had some little dust sands in them that made him uncomfortable. It was the effect of the war in Liberia, the IDF, went off on his face while he was saving one of his men and he was lucky to escape death himself.

The new appointment of Josey Igodalo as the Head of the new task force was to solve the kidnapped Diplomat's case was not a surprise to the majority of his peers, if there was anyone that could do it, he was and the president was hailed by the press for the appointment. He finally got it right this time, everyone said.

Josey Igodalo was recalled by the presidency from the Boko Haram infested Battalion in Maiduguri in the North East of Nigeria, to fill in the gap from the fired National Security adviser and IG it made his appointment imperious, even the critics of President Boniface's administration said Josey was the right man for the job.

The media made a field day of it in the last twenty-four hours with the sudden resignation of the two top Security Chiefs from the administration of President Boniface.

In the last two days, lots of rumors even went with it, some said, the IG Kosoko was the kidnapper himself, it was even rumored, that they found the missing Diplomat in his girlfriend's house on Maitama Sule Crescent which was why he was removed from the office and all these made the appointment of Major General Igodalo for the job tougher, and everyone expected him to perform magic or miracle or whichever comes first out of the two.

The Press talked of Igodalo's praise like a savior, his achievement and successes with the wars of freedom in Liberia, and Sierra Leone from Charles Taylor who murdered his people was something to behold.

From the early security briefing he had with the Chief of Staff, his mission and appointment would still be subjected to the ratification of the Senate. Dr. Hakeem, the Secretary to the Federal Government told him.

"We have enough trouble with the Senate already, we can't afford another scandal." He told General Igodalo

"I understand the concerns of the President." He replied.

"Just Hallo my office and we do the political press button for you on any issue that involves the Senate" He added.

"Thank you for that." He replied.

General Igodalo could still read the files, he could also meet with the staff, and that was about it, all other resources would be on hold, particularly, any financial spending which must be approved by the National Assembly. Those were the specific instruction from the Presidency.

Major General Igodalo assumed duty with his Personal Assistant Lt. Col. Azubuike, at the SSS office on Obasanjo Way earlier in the early hours of a Friday.

The old SSS office was an obscure building, with faded paint, unknown to the outside world; it had six-floor underground offices and seventy miles tunnel that extended to Lokoja.

The tunnel was built to protect the Presidency after the attack and a military coup of Major Okar against the dictator Military President of General Ibrahim Babangida in 1990, his then-personal assistant then, Col. Bello was killed by just a stroke of luck and it forced General Babangida who escaped being killed to relocate from Lagos to Abuja the new Federal Capital of Nigeria.

All the files on the Kidnapped Diplomat were dumped on Major General Igodalo's desk, he had asked for more information on Darley by the time he spent almost four hours reading through the reports, his findings concluded the guy must be more than just a Diplomat, he was probably a member of the FBI or US Homeland Security employed by United States of America government to do some dirty jobs outside the Consular offices.

The United States of America Consular office in Lagos had been helpful, they gave them time and several email conversations of Darley with Dolapo his contact in the Governor's office in Abeokuta and he asked his men to invite Dolapo for a meeting with him as soon as he hit Abeokuta next day.

General Igodalo could still recall his years in the City of Abeokuta as a young military officer after he was commissioned to serve with one of the oldest Battalions in the country. It was beautiful then and probably still was. He made lots of friends that helped his career growth and he was looking forward to reconnecting with some of them.

CHAPTER 31

𝕬beokuta. 2ⁿᵈ 𝕺ctober

𝕯olapo was a quiet and understanding man, he had received an invitation from the SSS office at Oke Imosan on Sagamu Road just as he was about to drive into his office Complex.

"Are you Dolapo?" A man who appeared like a military guy asked him.

"If it is not me, who do you think it should be?" He said with a sense of humor.

"I am Joshua from SSS, and my superiors would like to invite you for a meeting in connection with the missing Diplomat. "He flashed a badge at him.

"Give me a few minutes to clear my movement with my boss." He said.

"2 pm later in the day will be fine due to the urgency attached to it from the presidency, "He said.

"Okay," Dolapo said.

Did he just hear the SSS guy mentioned the Presidency?

Dolapo was worried. He was with Darley up to late in the night up to the time he was kidnapped, they had parted and promised to call back as soon as he got to Lagos and that was the last time he saw him. He never did, he heard the rest of the story on the Network News.

Dolapo headed straight to the Secretary to the Government office, hid direct boss a few minutes later he obtained clearance from the office of the SSG Dr. Fade on the invitation and as he drove towards the office of SSS he said a silent prayer, which bothers more on guardians than his innocence

As soon as Dolapo drove into the office of the SSS complex, he knew something was wrong, he sent a text message to his wife on his location in case he was unable to get out on time, the message did not go through. He resents it and again it came unsent. He heard stories of people that never made it back, and when he heard Major General Josey Igodalo was the new SSS Director he took it with mixed feelings.

Dolapo looked for a parking spot on the edge of the lot, which has always been his style; he loved to park his vehicle in a very conspicuous place to avoid hit and run that was always common in a busy lot. He found one at the tail end, he parked, and before he came out of his car, he did a sign of the cross like the Roman Catholic. He approached the Reception, it was a small office almost the size of a restroom with just a single chair for one visitor, he greeted the Receptionist first, who ignored his greetings, and almost out of the blues he asked him for hid identification.

"May I see your Driver's License or any picture ID you have sir" He said distractedly.

He gave it to him. The Receptionist held it as if he was touching a piece of a soiled toilet paper, he placed it under the light and whatever he was looking for, it appeared as if the license passed the lie test or something because his countenances changed.

"Please sit down here sir; the General will see you shortly." He said.

"Thank you, Officer," Dolapo said.

Dolapo sat down and he was thinking of the night he was with Darley at Ogun State Hotel before he was kidnapped, he had told him it was too late in the night to commute back to Lagos, and he was free to spend the night with him or take a room at the Hotel but he had refused.

"I have to be at work very early to attend a telephone conference in DC." He said.

"You have my telephone number in case you need me, just watch out for the potholes on that Express Road, if I were you, I would take Abeokuta Road. "He told him.

"I get this friend." He said.

"Call me as soon as you hit Lagos," Dolapo told him.

He watched him as he drove his Black BMW quietly towards the gate of the Hotel and as he turned right toward the night on the Sagamu Road. He dialed a number.

"He is on his way." He said.

"The General will see you now," The Receptionist said, it was more like a whisper. Dolapo stood up, he straightened up his tie and he followed the direction given to him.

"Take the elevator to the fifth floor, turn right, and move to the left, the fifth door on the right followed the passage to your right then you will see a door in blue color, turn the nob upright." The Receptionist had said.

Holy Moses! What a confusion with all the turnings, and whoever turns the nob of a door upright in the 21st century, they must be nuts here. He told himself.

Dolapo found the blue door he turned right, he found the nob, and he turned the nob upright, it opened, and he was looking directly at the man the whole country talked about with admiration. As he approached his desk, the General stood up and extended his hand to him, he noticed on his right the General was not alone, his Personal Assistant Lt. Col. Azubuike was taking notes or something, and both of them looked like the way had seen them on Television in the previous weeks.

"You must be Dolapo the friend of the Diplomat." He said.

"Yelp! I am the victim of his friendship, now the whole country knows me." Dolapo said.

"Please sit down; this is Lt Col Azubuike my PA. Just a few questions here and there for clarifications, I promise you, it will not be longer than necessary "He said.

"Have you written your Will already?" He said laughing.

"May I know why you said that General?" Dolapo asked.

"It is written all over your face, you looked like shit." He said. He had a broad smile on his face.

"I guess I am, General." He replied.

"You don't have to. We have already checked you out, from all your transactions with the Diplomat in the last three years, including your brother he assisted with the visa a few years ago, and all your investment including the money you sent to your mother in the village three weeks ago" General Igodalo said with that suspicious smile on his face.

"Humm," Dolapo said.

"As I told you, I will not look into the gay activities stuff between you and the Diplomat; we don't even want to embarrass the United States of America with that too if you can assist the agency with the details of how and why you were helping the Diplomat to get in touch with the Oracle?" He said with a straight face.

"You knew the relationship between us?" Dolapo asked.

"We are the Government don't forget that, but it is okay, it shows we have lower body connections with the Americans with your bedroom activities." He said with a big smile on his face.

"Please don't let my wife know about this." He pleaded.

"We don't mess with people's lifestyle unless you refuse to cooperate; I think that gays stuff carries 14 years jail term in the country, if we have to use it on you, then I guess the President signed the Law a few months ago." He said it more like a threat.

Dolapo was deflated, all his 25 years in the Service of Ogun State government and his next promotion to the Permanent Secretary would be gone in the wind, and 14 years in jail in those filthy jail houses in Nigeria is not what he was looking forward to. He started singing like the cannery Bird.

"Darley received instruction from DC to contact the Oracle on a guy with an altered mental status issue in the state of Tennessee and to facilitate the meeting I had to arrange the meeting with the Oracle." He began.

"When was your first meeting with the Oracle?" Col. Azubuike asked.

"About two weeks ago," Dolapo answered.

"Were you physically there or you just facilitated the meeting?" He asked.

"I was at the first meeting not the second." He said.

"How much was involved?" He asked

"I heard something about Half a million dollars." He said.

"In cash or bond?" He asked.

"Cash only." He said.

"Did you meet the contact from America when he came to Abeokuta with his girlfriend?" General Igodalo asked.

"I am not aware of his visit." He said.

"Are you aware he came with a bodyguard who died in Lagos Airport restroom of snakebite?" Col Azubuike asked.

"I am not aware of it." He answered.

"Are you aware of the SSS staff that was knocked down in the hotel also got stuffed in the mouth with money in his mouth when he woke up?" He said.

"I am not sure of what you are saying," He said.

"What then are you aware of?" he said.

Dolapo kept quiet.

"Are you aware you collected the balance of the money from the Diplomat and you deposited it into accountant 342347890 with Oceanic Bank two days ago?" Col Azubuike asked.

Dolapo kept quiet.

"Maybe I need to be talking to Mrs. Dolapo instead of you." General Igodalo said.

"What do you want from me?" He pleaded.

"The Diplomat went back to Lagos in a Black BMW as soon as he left you in the Hotel. Right!" He asked.
"Yes." He said.

"Was it a rented car or his car?" He asked.

"I do not know," Dolapo said.

"Do you want to reconsider your statement on this car issue?" Col. Azubuike asked.

"I have nothing to do with the car." He said.

"I see. Who owned Dolaps Car Rentals in Lagos?" He asked.

Dolapo's mouth was very dry by now, he licked his lips.

"I think you will need a bottle of water." Col Azubuike said.

He stood up, he opened the little refrigerator by his desk, and he brought two bottles of Eva medium size water bottles, he pushed one of them towards Dolapo.

"I noticed you were sweating; I have a box of tissue on the table." He said.

Dolapo took two sheets of the paper napkins on the table, he wiped the sweat off his forehead and he threw it into the trash basket beside him.

The next question took him off his balance.

"When was the last time you went to Eriki Odofin village?" He asked.

"Last month." He answered with a frown on his face.

"Who drove the black Honda Ridgeline 2004 model to the village two nights ago?" He asked.

Dolapo kept quiet.

General Igodalo pushed the button under his desk and two heavy-set looking officers came up.

"You guys will go to the country home of Dolapo at Eriki Village, you will search and come back here in the next three hours because I will be waiting." He instructed.

"Dolapo, I will have to keep you here until the guys come back. Do you have a Lawyer because I think you are going to need one?" General Igodalo said.

He was no longer laughing his face was as cold as ice blocks; he looked like the General he used to see on the television.

"Am I under arrest or what?" Dolapo asked.

"You want me to read the charges for you? He said.

"Humm," Dolapo said.

"Extortions, Kidnapping, and gay activities, the Press will love it by tomorrow morning, now you know you are under arrest." He said smoothly as if they were talking Buddies. The two men led Dolapo away into the detention room.

"You are allowed to make a phone call to your wife or Attorney," one of the guys said before the door was slammed on behind him.

CHAPTER
32

Eriki Odofin village

Eriki Odofin village was on the outskirt of Lagos Express Road. It was the spot the Diplomat was kidnapped. He was about to turn left, on the sharp road that led to the Express road, before he saw what appeared to look like a Police roadblock, he slowed down and three men in a police uniform approached his car with guns, he thought they were regular policemen until one of them mentioned his name.

"Are you Darley?" He asked.

"Yes. How may I help you, officer?" He said.

"One of the ways to help is to get your Black Ass out of the car before I wrap these bullets into your Coconut head," He said harshly.

Darley immediately felt this could be a stickup, no reasonable police would use those dirty words to address anyone, he had to be careful, and he complied with all their instructions until they whisked him away into a waiting van and the other one drove his car behind them.

It has been three days since he was locked up in the hidden place by these kidnappers, he had no contact with the outside world, and the food was greasy and smells horrible.

"What type of food is this? Darley asked.

"Why do you ask?" The guy next to him asked.

"How do I eat this food now?" He asked.

"You open your two lips, and your teeth and place the food in between your big ass mouth, not your eyes because it will burn you or you can't do that?" He said sarcastically.

Darley wondered why he engaged the guy in any conversation at all, few hours later they were lined up and trooped out into a waiting eighteen-wheeler vehicle, about the van, they were all chained to the back seat of the truck, about fifteen of them, the stench of strong body odor was horrible, and a few hours ago, one of them had died when the truck driver of the vehicle was about to move, that alone forced the driver and the other two guards to tarry a bit.

Darley raised his head; he looked through the pee hole on the side of the truck he noticed two approaching vehicles with police siren light flashing on it. One of the guards yelled to his Buddies

"We have companies." He said.

He jumped out of the truck and ran towards the bush, the other two followed the fourth, one was not so lucky before he was apprehended by the team of police and SSS.

They opened the truck they found fifteen hostages including the emaciated Diplomat.

The rescue was hailed by the International press and comity of nations in the western world. It improved the opinion polls of the two Presidents, in Africa, Dr. Boniface finally earned the respect of his people and the opposition party the APC had to go back to the drawing board to find a new strategy to weaken his presidency, in the United States of America, President Chris Candlewood opinion poll went up, the stock market went up and the Republican Party waited for another opportunity to get at the Presidency through his nominee for the Supreme Court.

CHAPTER

33

When Patrick returned from Africa from his meeting with the Oracle, he noticed he had given him the tiniest bottle one could imagine and black soap. He was surprised the solution to his brother's problem was just a cream made out of sheer butter which the Oracle asked him to mix with the armpit hair of PJ, who must take a bath with it late in the night at the junction leading to his Mission house in Memphis Tennessee.

The bathwater and the towel in a bowl must be thrown into a running river, not a stream or Lake but a fast running river; he said, and everything must be done by midnight.

The most important thing was how to get PJ discharged under AMA against medical advice to be able to perform the simple ritual of a bath. He planned his trip for Terrell Texas the following day. His work was suffering, and the Boss in Chicago the Corporate office was already complaining, however, his record as the most untainted staff of the group made him irreplaceable.

There was no direct flight to Terrell in Texas, all flights stopped at DFW International Airport in Dallas Texas and a chartered flight could only fly to Kaufman in Texas the rest of the trip would have to be made on the road on Highway 80 with the most active Police Patrol in East Texas.

Patrick flew to Dallas through Lovefied Airport on Mockingbird Avenue; he had called the Advantage Car Hire services for a black Mercedes Benz. It was neatly packed and cleaned for him when he picked the car up, he drove through Mockingbird lane in Dallas Texas to Highway 35 East, through 175 until he got to 635 North and the roads were smooth and wide until he got to Highway 80 was even wider. He could not resist the need to press more on the gas pedal, he did, and he was doing between 70 to 80 miles per hour.

Police Sergeant Vitkong was a Vietnam veteran, who later joined the Police force of Kaufman Texas; he had no ambition than to be on the road. He had eagle eyes, and he could smell crimes from a very long distance, two things about him being separated him from his peers, he has never arrested any criminal that got freed in any Court in Kaufman Texas, they called him Razor Blade and he gnawed tobacco in a very distasteful manner.

Officer Vitkong had been waiting in the police unmarked car, in the obscure sharp corner on Highway 80 when a black Mercedes Benz with a rental plate number zoomed past him, and his radar cut a speed of 100 miles per hour on a highway with 55 mph speed limit. He turned on the flashing serine light and both cars engaged in speed chase until the driver of the Black Mercedes Benz stopped.

Police Officer Vitkong parked his gadget-controlled vehicle directly behind the Black Mercedes, he turned on the HQ transmission box, and the camera began a recording transmitted to all the police control, units within 100 miles radius. He pulled out his flashlight and with his hand resting on his gun, he approached the Black car and he was rolling and chewing his tobacco in his mouth.

Patrick knew from his days in Brooklyn how to handle Policemen and women. Immediately Police officer Vitkong approached his car he already knew what to say or how to handle Texas active and overexcited police officers.

"Boy oh Boy I have been waiting for a speedrunner like you over here for a long time." He said.

"I hope I got here faster than you could imagine." He said with a broad smile on his face.

Sergeant Vitkong looked at him briefly, and he too smiled.

"Boy oh Boy, I like your sense of humor, I will just give a warning ticket if I do catch you again, and you will not thank your stars, I promise you." He said.

"Thank you. Officer." Patrick said.

Few miles more he would be in Terrell and should be able to get his brother out of the mental Hospital. He noticed a Texaco Gas station as soon as he hit the road, he pulled over for coffee and to fill up his gas tank and time to use the bathroom.

By the time he walked out of the Gas Station he noticed his side mirror had been vandalized, he never asked any question he drove straight to Terrell.

In the day room in the Mental hospital were different types of patients, with lots of different diagnoses, and each displayed unusual behaviors, one of them was Piston Parico from Puerto Rico and his questions bother everyone around him, sometimes he would ask anyone who cares to listen to him if they were Jewish or Catholic, in most cases he would ask if they were mean.

Piston Parico sat beside another patient who had been overmedicated. As soon Patrick sat down the question from Parico surprised him.

"Are you Catholic?" Parico asked.

"No. I am not." Patrick replied.

"Umm." He murmured.

"Are you Jewish?" Parico asked.

"No. I am not." Patrick replied.

"Umm." He murmured.

"Are you meaning?" He asked him

"No. I am not." Patrick replied.

"Umm," He murmured.

Patrick noticed each time he answered Parico he just said umm, something must be wrong with him. What am I even saying? He questioned himself,

"Am not in a Gad damn mental institution?"

Opposite his chair was another patient laughing very loud, the one on his left who had introduced himself to him as Angelo said.

"I want whatever medication she had this morning," Angelo said.

"What do you mean?" Patrick asked.

"With the way she was smiling and laughing." He said.

"That was funny," Patrick said, and surprisingly he too was still laughing when his brother came in with the Nurse.

"I am Tammy, the Case Manager for your brother. You must be Patrick." She said.

"I am. How are you doing?" He said.

"Doing just fine." She said.

"How soon can we get him out?" He asked.

PJ never altered a word. He was quiet with inquisitive eyes.

"Of you would have to have a meeting with the Social Worker and DN before his release could be effected, the Administrator of the facility had already given the go-ahead with Doctor's approval, the rest is just paperwork." She said.

Two hours later, he was on his way to DFW International Airport with his brother and Nurse which will be paid for out of pocket, the Obama care or ACA program did not cover out of state special treatment.

CHAPTER

34

The ritual and spiritual bath for PJ to free him of the spiritual curse was immediately fixed for midnight as instructed by the Oracle, the male Nurse Reggie Maxwell was to be paid over one hundred thousand dollars for this unusual assignment at the unfriendly hour of the night and it must take place in front of the mission house, in the way the Oracle had directed.

Patrick knew by now never to outsmart the Oracle with the death of his Bodyguard Stern Marco in Africa everything must be followed by the book.

Patrick had used his influence to obtain a special permit from the City to close the street down and it was very easy to conduct the bath away from the prying eyes of commuters not because it was a busy street, it was not. Just to prevent any eventualities as directed by the Oracle, he had warned that only the Nurse must witness the event, not even Patrick otherwise, he might have to go back to Africa to see him again, and that he dreaded.

It was done as planned, the Nurse, Reggie Maxell was diligent with it. He washed PJ down from his head to his toes, with the black soap in the bowl, he scrubbed him up with the new white towel from the toes up to the head not the usual way of the head to toes, and it was the way the Oracle directed.

Reggie lotion PJ's body down up with the shear buttercream then he stepped a dazed PJ out of the bowl; into his wheelchair just outside the mission house gate, he poured seven cowries and fifteen guinea pepper into the bowl. He did not miss the guidelines, he followed everything as instructed.

Reggie moved everything including the bowl into the back of his truck without looking back or saying anything to PJ on the Wheelchair behind him, he headed for the Mississippi River as he drove through downtown Memphis to complete the ritual. It was only a fifteen minutes' drive, everything was looking like easy money for Reggie and the road was lonely with not many vehicles around. He felt good and relieved. What easy money he thought!

When he got to the bank of River Mississippi, he stopped the truck, but he kept the ignition key on the truck. He waited for about five minutes, still, there was no one around, he felt a little bit of cold inside him, just a little bit not too much to stop him from completing the assignment, somehow something was crawling on his skin, and he almost canceled the whole deal on second thought, he could feel something unusual.

A few minutes later, Reggie without his shoes on steeped out of his truck with the bowl filled up with the ritual concoction and after bathwater of PJ, he walked towards the river on the sharp sands, he thought as he walked he heard some footsteps behind him.

Could it be his imagination? But Patrick had warned him not to look back otherwise, what happened to PJ might happen to him and that would be just too bad. He was scared by now. He had thought it would be just a simple activity but something was telling him, he might be getting more than he bargained for and he wished he had asked for more than the one hundred thousand dollars a night assignment.

Reggie knew why he took this unusual job which had nothing to do with his professional career as a Registered Nurse, or who could get a license to carry rituals in America at the very odd hours? He questioned his judgment on why he got himself involved. But he needed the money to pay off his student loan, his car notes, his two-bedroom Condo house in Texas, and to pay for a new car for his wife Cheryl who had threatened to leave him if he was unable to make a decision on what she wanted or not.

Cheryl wanted the new Honda Civics car and she was going to get it with or without him. He noticed she had opened an account on Match.com in search of new admirers and she upgraded her profile photographs on the Facebook page. It was not a good sign.

He planned to keep his wife.

Reggie had two things that scared him to death, he hated snakes in any form, black, yellow, and short or long, just any snake even a mere sight of earthworm could remind of snakes, and the touch of sharp sands on a barefoot walk and he had no preference for both. It was the way and manner a snake that killed his mother in Tampa City in the State of Florida.

Reggie was sixteen years then, he had dreamt of a massive snake attack the previous night after he watched a snake movie, and he got up in the middle of the night from his bed to go to the bathroom, when he noticed his Mom's door was wide open, he called her. She did not answer, he entered her room, he found a big black snake around her neck, and she was foaming in the mouth.

Reggie ran out in the middle of the night, barefooted to seek help, the nearest neighbor was almost half a mile away, as he was running, he felt the sharp pain of the sand in between his toes, his neighbor did not open the door and he was dangerously harassed by his dog, by the time he eventually, opened the door and called for paramedical, his single mother was long dead.

That was twenty years ago.

Reggie stepped into the cold water of the Mississippi River, with the ritual bowl, it was not a friendly temperature, he had no socks on, and the sharpness of the sand was biting, he moved ahead until the river got to his knees, he lowered the bowl into the flowing Mississippi river; he gently gave it a push, to his surprised something unusual happened.

What was that?

What seemed like the three hands under the river suddenly appeared and the hands guided the bowl to the center of the river to his surprise, the three hands and the bowl disappeared or submerged; the whole scene was like a trance but it was not a trance, it was real.

Reggie ran like a fool to his car, he was breathing heavily by the time he opened the driver side door of his truck, he dipped his right hand into his pocket for the ignition key, it was nowhere to be found, his pocket was empty, and he recollected, he had left it on the truck itself, as he looked up he saw the key, he sat down and he was about to start the engine when he noticed his seat was cold and wet like the inside of a deep freezer.

Whatever it was on the seat that made it wet made a slight movement under his butt, he turned the interior light on, he could not believe it, he was sitting on a snake, the black mamba, with its tongue spitting out like a little dragon before he could say, Jack Robinson, he was struck twice in the butt before he could do anything, the snake which was now at the same eye level with him struck him twice again on eyes and twice again on the nose.

The Black Mamba snake crawled out of his truck and it went in the direction of the river, it raised its head as if to congratulate itself for a mission accomplished, as it slides into the river, its head was still showing, as it moved in the same direction like the bowl, the same three hands appeared the snake curled itself and the hands and both submerged into the river.

Reggie could no longer move his hands, he was weak and tired, and he was sweating profusely, from the corner of his right eye, and he looked at his Cell phone, it was ringing and it kept on ringing, but he could not even bring himself up to pick it up. It was from his wife Cheryl. He knew he was never going to keep her or pay off his student loan, he felt the sharp pain inside his left chest, it was then he realized he had been used as a human scarifies for the mental and spiritual problem of PJ and it was too late for him.

Still, in pain, Reggie reminisced the last few hours of his mother, with the snake around her neck and the bites on her face and the sharp sand between his toes, when he was looking for help to save his mother, and now helplessly, in the same pain from the effect of the venom of the snake poison bite, he saw his mother with the gloomy look sorrowfully done on her with a dry smile, which had eaten deeply into her after his father left them. She was no longer biter, she looked peaceful with herself, she extended her hands to him, he found himself walking towards her and Reggie knew he was going to be with her, the only person who genuinely loved him.

A few minutes later, all alone, he was foaming in the mouth, his eyes rolled back as his skin turned ashy, the snake poison gradually moved up more into the four ventricles of the valves of his heart, his heart shot down. He died by the River Mississippi.

Immediately, Reggie died by the Mississippi River, the unexpected happened. PJ instantly recovered from the Wheelchair, he stood up, his eyes were cleared, it was as if he came out of comatose in the ICU of a Teaching Hospital, he walked through the mission gate straight into the waiting hands of his brother Peter, he asked for water and his favorite Taco Mexican food.

Patrick who had watched the whole scene by his brother's side was relieved. It was a mission accomplished, suddenly, he remembered what the Oracle said, about whoever carried the ritual to the river would go through, and he had said,

"Only mother luck could prevent the carrier from any catastrophe." He said.

What happened to Reggie he wondered? He was paid all the hundred thousand dollars upfront which was also the instruction from the Oracle.

"Do not attempt to set your eyes on the carrier again because if you do, a lot might happen." The Oracle had warned.

Patrick did not until he opened the Memphis Herald Newspapers two days later did he know what happened to

Reggie Maxell, the photograph of the battered face of Reggie stared him in the face and it was the news on the front page of the newspaper.

"................Male Nurse 37 with hundred thousand dollars cash found dead on what appeared to be snake Bite in the Butt and on the nose and eyes at Mississippi River and the news said further that the matter was still under investigation by the City Police......."

Patrick knew it could be traced to him, he was the last person who saw Reggie alive and he even brought him from Texas to Tennessee, he was not ready for any interrogations from the police, which would not look good with his organization. He placed a call to Mayor James, a member of the Mafia itself, his job was to direct the City Police to look elsewhere other than Patrick. But he was worried, about the snake, if there was any relationship or snake attack between Stern Marco his bodyguard who died in Africa, and then Reggie.

The last instruction from the Oracle was for him to recover the tiny ring on the left toe of Gina the wife of his brother, he must break it into two equal parts, along with the empty case of the Shear butter he gave him to rub on PJ, they must be shipped back through DHL to him in Africa within 21 days after the recovery of his brother, the package of recovery treatment would then be fully accepted by the gods in the shrine, the Oracle had said.

The Oracle did not tell him, the repercussions of his failure of not sending back the package, whatever it was he was not ready to find out also.

He had to do it.

CHAPTER
35

Federal FBI Office TN

The Federal FBI had just opened a special case note on Nurse Reggie, who died of snakebite by the Mississippi River, they traced his work history, he had no license to even practice as a Male Nurse in the state of Tennessee, his License was suspended two years ago for unethical works, however, until his death, he was a staff of Terrell mental Hospital in Texas as ordinary Certified Nursing Assistant.

Why did he end up at the bank of the River Mississippi at the ugly hour of the night? The weather was not friendly to even warrant any bath or swimming, the report traced his footprints from the truck to the river, one of them appeared to be steady, the second was done in a hurry as he ran back to his truck.

Did he encounter something from the river?

Wagman thought his last few years with the FBI would be freed of murder cases, however; the Pinnacle Pentecostal Church case had expanded more than he could imagine, the report said, PJ had been discharged AMA against medical advice from Terrell Hospital, and he was back in his house in Memphis.

Surprisingly, Wagman observed from the report on his desk that Reggie, the male Nurse found by the Mississippi River had also accompanied PJ and an unnamed individual from Texas to Memphis Tennessee five days ago, it could not have been a coincidence, there must have been a correlation or collaboration of events, that, he intended to find out, and he planned to pay PJ and his brother Patrick a visitation but he would have to interrogate the Administrator of Terrell mental institution first.

He placed a call to the Justice Department in Texas and the City of Terrell Police Department finally he called Judge Woodrow to obtain a search warrant for his team.

CHAPTER

36

𝕿errell 𝕳ospital

𝕯r. James Baxton was glad everything was over; the management had finally accepted his resignation, the final date of his disengagement from the services of the Hospital, and the sendoff party was slated for Friday which would come up in the next twenty-four hours. The Board had informed him a sendoff party in his honor had been arranged and they expected him to attend the party with his family and three other friends.

Dr. James Baxton had directed his Personal Assistant Marie to send all visitors to Dr. Vasquez his successor, and his desk was getting lighter as the days of his retirement from service was getting closer, he had a smile on his face, it would be fine he told himself, as he was looking forward to his final exit from Terrell, his wife had suggested they should move to Florida and on top of their list was the City of Tampa with little or no hurricane year in year out, besides, the weather was friendlier than the hot State of Texas.

Dr. Baxton was still thinking of what his life would be after several years in the midst of those with mental issues, sometimes, he wondered if those working with these mentally retarded patients had not been infected with the sickness of those they treat too. Marie his Personal Assistant pops up her head by the door.

"You have a visitor Mr. Baxton," He said

"Is it official?" Baxton asked.

"Yes but." He was still struggling with his words when Baxton said."

"What part of simple instruction you couldn't understand, I said all visitors to Dr. Vasquez," He said in annoyance.

"I understand Dr. Baxton. But I think you need to see this guy." She said.

"Where is it from?" He asked

"He said he is from the Government," She said.

"The government? He asked.

"Yes." She replied.

"Like IRS or FBI?" Baxton asked.

"He does not look like a Tax guy to me, Dr. Baxton; besides, he had a gun in his shoulder pack side pant." She said.

"How did you know he had a gun?" He asked.

"Dr. Baxton, don't forget I am from Texas." She said.

"Ok. I will see him" Baxton said.

Baxton's mouth turned sour, he knew he had no pending Tax cases to fix in his job; he hadn't been on any fraud list and was still thinking if a new allegation was found because he could not think of any at the moment.

When the visitor pushed open the office door, he knew something was wrong with the alibi he might be thinking of, the man from the government approached him and he flashed his FBI Barge at him, Baxton heart skipped.

Was he under arrest or what?

Wagman mustache spread all over his face, and his eyes looked greenish like a deadly snake, he was not on a social visit, and he did not even border to shake the hand Dr. Baxton extended to him, Baxton knew everything did not appear friendly from the beginning.

"I understand Friday will be your last day on this facility. Right!" He asked.

"I am looking forward to it, with all pleasure." He said.

"I am afraid, that pleasure has been suspended," Wagman said with a contempt smile on his lips.

"By whose authority will that be?" Baxton asked.

Wagman ignored him while he just cares about his FBI Barge.

"What is your relationship with Patrick and PJ his brother?" He asked at the same time, he ignored Baxton's last remarks.

"Just a professional relationship." He said.

"That professional relationship included Reggie you recommended to escort PJ back to Memphis. Right? He said dryly.

"Reggie needed help and I allowed him to earn a couple of Bucks," He said

"So that couple of bucks amounts to one hundred thousand dollars?" He quarried.

"It depends. I have no ideas about the details of the transaction." He said.

Dr. Baxton's throat was dried, he needed something to drink and the more he looked at Wagman's greenish eyes the more he felt like using the bathroom.

"You have no idea of the details. Right! And you got fifty thousand dollars from the deal?" He asked.

"I am not following you, officer," he said.

"Let me refresh your memory. You deposited fifty thousand dollars into the college fund of your son through your wife's account" He explained.

Baxton kept quiet, he was thinking maybe he should involve his Attorney or not, the right side of his head was pounding as if it would explode out.

"Maybe I should be talking to your wife too or you still want to stick to your purely professional funny talk?" He asked.

Baxton felt it would be hard on him if his wife ever knew the details of what Wagman was asking of him. He might not even retire to Tampa's City, from the way Wagman was talking, he felt he was setting him up for retirement in the Federal Prison in San Antonio Texas, and from what he heard about the place it was not pretty at all.

"I will need all the medical records of PJ from his first day here in this facility and the name of the Doctor who did his evaluation and diagnosis," Wagman said.

"That will be against HIPPA regulation unless you have a signed order from a Judge." Baxton managed to sound confident as if he scored a victory over the FBI agent.

"I have one here already," Wagman said.

"My Secretary will give you all the documentation in the Pdf document." He said.

Immediately Wagman stood up, two Police officers came in he gave Baxton a dry smile.

"You are under arrest in the complicity of facts leading to the death of Reggie, and money laundering. You have the right to remain silent and whatever you say from now will be used against you, you can seek the use of your Attorney or we provide you with one." He said.

The two police officers handcuffed Baxton; his Personal Assistant Marie who just handed over the medical records of PJ to Wagman looked in a bewilder surprise just as Dr. Baxton was led off to a waiting police car outside.

CHAPTER

37

PJ was still in a very deep sleep in his bedroom and his brother Patrick was going through all his papers in the Study room, he was reading the various get well cards from the Congregations some of them had unprintable words on them, they were even bold enough to put in their first name on the cards.

"Motherfucker, you can go to hell." Batista

"Spinning dick Pastor," Mario wrote.

"Go rot in hell, PJ." a signed name Augusto Marlon.

"Did you show your foreskin to the MR too in Terrell?" Antonio asked.

"Can you show us your foreskin again on Sunday because I will be there?" She signed her name Josephine.

Patrick wondered if and how his brother would react to all the ugly and abusive words on the greeting cards. He knew PJ could not handle that problem alone and he did not want to bother Jean after the scary visit to Africa; it was a nightmare for her.

Jean did not say anything when he knocked down the State Security Service guy in the Hotel, in West Africa and she had watched him with amazement chiefly on how he stocked the money into his mouth, everything had happened too fast, in all, she never quivered or sacred, she was cool and collected.

Jean had gone back to work in DC after two days with him, the journey to Africa to her was a disaster, and they planned to meet for dinner next week, he hoped he could get his brother organized or situated before the flight to DC.

Patrick was still deep in thought by the bedside of PJ when he heard the footsteps, he pulled the cards away into the desk drawer and he went for his gun in his hip pocket. He stood up and moved closer to the door, the footsteps kept coming toward the room, he peeped through the keyhole, the steps were from Gina, he opened the door slightly enough to see her full body, she had on her, a gown that exposed her legs and her toes, it was then he remembered what the Oracle said about the ring on her left foot.

Gina walked past Patrick and he could smell the fragrance of her perfume. She went straight to the chair very close to the bedroom, she did not even say a word or acknowledge his presence, it was her home, besides, she could remember how Patrick had persuaded her to marry his brother, after several years of sleeping with her.

Gina wondered why she allowed her life to be controlled in the way Patrick arranged it. But she knew better than that, Patrick with a wave of a hand could destroy her.

It was like a trance after PJ had recovered from the mental illness and lost in space, more like it never really happened to him. Everything was closer to waking up from a trance or nightmares or a Biblical miracle from the New Testament.

The last PJ could remember was the day the Chairman, Board of Trustees of the Church died, and when he walked to the pulpit to preach. It was the way it happened; Patrick told him. The shame was too much for him, he wept just as Patrick held him. Gina did not say a word. It was like the two brothers never existed in her world.

"But what really happened to me?" He asked.

"No one could tell, but whatever it was could not have been freed of voodoo attack," Patrick said.

By the time PJ heard the details of what happened and how he brought out his manhood in the Church, he felt bad;

he knew he had to do the most honorable stuff. He would have to send his letter of resignation to the Board of Trustees.

PJ could neither bring himself to look at Gina in the eyes nor how she felt after he had exposed the top family secret to the congregation on a Sunday, throughout the conversation and detailed analysis of everything was controlled.

Gina who had kept quiet was deflated by everything, her pride and dignity were gone and it could be seen that the marriage was over for them, with Patrick who brokered the relationship at the beginning presiding on how and why it should be ended.

The divorce would be announced to friends and family members next weekend after the modalities of assets and liabilities were worked out by the divorce lawyers and stakeholders.

In the divorce papers, PJ painfully signed his rights over the Church to Gina. It was like losing a baby to him, the Church was his life, but he knew when to move on. The second day, PJ was transported to Mexico through the vehicle arranged by his brother and as soon as he got to Mexico he was given a first-class ticket for a flight to Cayman Island.

Two days after PJ left Gina with Patrick, she had secretly met with John the ex-husband of Tina, at a restaurant in Downtown Memphis, she had willingly given all the documentation and codes to all the secret joint accounts and the shares of Tina Brown everything was amicably settled. She kept faith with all the agreement with Tina, even in death she respected her friend and her wishes on how the investment should be placed in trust for Samuel her only son.

John was not surprised at the development, the Oracle had said everything would be given to him or Samuel, he longed to see him, but Oracle would not pick up his calls, he had said, six months after which everything would be fine, the gods would give clearance for him to see the Oracle. And he waited.

In two weeks Gina would become the first female Pastor of Pinnacle Pentecostal Church. She still had the ring on her toes, and most of the nights she dreamt of being chased by snakes.

Did she give the ring on her toes to Patrick?

CHAPTER
38

𝕴mplausibly, one of the last conditions from the Oracle was the recovery of the ring on the left toe of Gina. After the meeting last night with his brother PJ, Patrick had invited Gina for a dinner, and he planned to discuss the possibility of recovering the ring on her toe from her. She had agreed to meet him on one condition Patrick would not revisit the disgraceful events in Church which deflated her ego.

Patrick sat at the side corner of Korana Restaurant; he was sipping his wine and casually looking at the women as they came into the restaurant to meet their dates and as some came in and out of the restaurant.

It usually started with greetings, a hug, and a lighter kiss, the process was the same, the performance determined if the relationship was deeper than a causal relationship.

In the same manner, he gave Gina a light kiss on the cheek just as she came into the Restaurant and they went straight to business. He concluded despite the departure of his brother for Mexico, the healing process of PJ would not be completed if the ring on her left toe could not be retrieved and shipped back to Africa.

Gina listened with amazement and how Patrick could allow himself to be controlled methodical mambo jumbles stuff from Africa, but if only the ring would be all it would take to see PJ through, she was ready to do it as long as the divorce decree would scale through. She needed a break from PJ and his brother, unknown to Patrick, the rings were two, and whatever she would be giving Patrick would be just one of them.

Gina removed the ring straight from her toe and she watched as Patrick placed it in his side pocket. Patrick was happy, for the first time in the last six weeks he was smiling, and he hugged her.

Patrick used the happy moment to inform her he was taking his relationship further up the ladder with Jean he would be getting married in Las Vegas.

Two days after, he sent through DHL, the tiny bottle, the leftover of the shear buttercream, and ring to the Oracle in Africa along with an additional five hundred thousand dollars to complete the healing process.

CHAPTER

39

𝕿wo years after Charles Wagman returned to Memphis after his retirement, he was shot in the head with the same gun that killed Mayor Charles according to the FBI report. Who shot him was clandestine to the Agency? He was a good staff and diligent in his responsibilities the report said.

The FBI had carried out a massive arrest for all the Board of Trustees of Pinnacle Church. It took the Bureau two years to wrap up investigations, Gina the ex-wife of PJ's and all the Board of Trustees were all charged for massive fraud and prostitution in the public place.

The court under Federal Judge Jones Brownville found them all guilty of fraud and were all sentenced to various terms. However, PJ who not even in the country was suspiciously found innocent under the influence of the spirit of Jezebel, the first un-cited case in the history of the United States Legal system, the truth was his brother took care of the Judge. Gina too was cleared of all charges as doctored by Patrick; it was his promise to her.

PJ retired to Cayman Island to enjoy the loot his brother had kept away for him, few months in the Cayman Islands, he met Rocio a beautiful and charming lady from Colombia, within two years, they had a son, and PJ named the boy, Samuel just like the son he never claimed from Tina.

Somehow ten years after, out of nowhere, an 18-year-old teenager walked through his lawn, he watched the young man from the window, he looked familiar and his gait was similar to his brother Patrick, the young guy knocked on his door, he opened the door, his smiles favors that of Tina, he was Samuel, the son he never claimed from Tina, he opened the door for him to come in, his son was finally home.

Somehow, he looked at the left toe of Samuel who had joined him in the swimming later in the evening; he saw on his left toe the same ring as what his ex-wife had several years back.

Gina was well into a juggling busy and hectic day by the time she settled in her private life in the Mission house of the Pinnacle gospel International. It has been tough than she expected, particularly on how to prepare sermons and attend to the administrative needs of the Church.

It was like everything rested on her shoulder, and it was since the Board of Trustee was dissolved and the need to find a replacement was imminent. She prayed for support and guidance.

It was the first month after the final divorce decree was released to her, she was about to start the sermon when two police officers in uniform walked into the Church, at first she thought they wanted to spend some time with the Lord, but they kept on moving toward the altar and her heart skipped.

Madame Gina." The one in dark glasses said.

"Yes. Pastor Gina PJ." Gina corrected.

"Do you know former Mayoral Charles' He asked?

"He was the Chairman of Trustees of our Church," She said.

"We have a reason to suspect you have something to do with the death." FBI Assistant Director, Charles Wagman for South Unit." He said.

Gina was arrested and charged for the murder of Chairman Board of Trustee and Charles Wagman, the was Gun was found in the basement of the mission house with the same gun same serial number.

The City of Memphis was amazed at the charges on Gina for the murder of Mayor Jackson; the court process lasted for six months. She was found guilty and sentenced to 24 years imprisonment without parole. Six months into her sentence she was found dead of snakebite in her Cell with a ring in her mouth, the spared one she failed to hand over to Patrick to ship to Africa.

Somewhere, in Africa, the Oracle was pouring Libation and performing his ritual as he was preparing to return to the United States of America.

Did he return to America?

AUTHOR'S

NOTE

This is a work of fiction only, it is not a resemblance to any living or dead person story, this story is purely the imagination of this author.

ABOUT THE AUTHOR

Dr. Zents K. Sowunmi is the founder of several charities in Africa and the USA, the author of several books namely "The *Vulture and the Vulnerable*," "*Unequally Yoking*," "*the Covenant-breakers*" The *Politics of manipulation since 1976*," including "*The secrets of Gabriel* "are some of his books.*

Sowunmi was a former Staff of the United States Department of Defense, Warrior Transition Battalion (WBT), and Fort Bliss Texas. He lives in his quiet Colonial Beach House in Long Island, Mastic Beach, New York, United States of America. **Zents Sowunmi** is also a titled High Chief and is referred to as Bada Tayese of Egbaland in Africa.

Do not miss these exciting books from this bestselling Author

ZENTS KUNLE SOWUNMI

The Vultures and the Vulnerable

ISBN 9781936739172

❖ *President Obama: Hero or Villain of Capitalism?*

ISBN 9781478230456

❖ *Ogun State: Policy of Manipulation since 1976*

ISBN 9781936739240

❖ *Before the Journey Became Home*

ISBN 9780615302621

❖ *100 ways to Laugh*

ISBN 9781936739172

❖ *Cien Maneras de Reir*

ISBN 9781936739004

❖ *What happened to Our Democracy?*

ISBN 9781936739110

❖ *The Secrets of Gabriel*

ISBN 97819367394445

Coming soon!!!

❖ The Return of the Oracle (Unequally Yoking Part two)

ISBN 9781936739172

❖ The Remaking of the Caliphate

ISBN 9781936739172

❖ The Covenant Breakers

ISBN 9781936739172

❖ The Mischievous Widow

ISBN 9781936739172

Order copies of this author's books directly from

www.kpcbooks.com

KORLOKI

PUBLISHERS

INC.

NEW YORK

USA

ZENTS K SOWUNMI